D0425632

Elmwood Park Branch
550 Chene
Detroit, MI 48207

APR   2013

EL

when the night whispers

when the night whispers

SAVANNA WELLES

st. martin's press
new york

This is a work of fiction. All of the characters, organizations, and events portrayed in this novel are either products of the author's imagination or are used fictitiously.

WHEN THE NIGHT WHISPERS.
Copyright © 2013 by Valerie Wilson Wesley. All rights reserved.
Printed in the United States of America. For information, address
St. Martin's Press, 175 Fifth Avenue, New York, N.Y. 10010.

www.stmartins.com

Design by Anna Gorovoy

ISBN 978-0-312-67571-4 (hardcover)
ISBN 978-1-250-02339-1 (e-book)

First Edition: February 2013

10 9 8 7 6 5 4 3 2 1

for janilynn

acknowledgments

I'd like to thank my agent, Faith Hampton Childs, for her belief and encouragement in this new venture, and my editors, Monique Patterson and Holly Blanck, for their assistance and support. And, of course, as always—much thanks to my family.

when the night whispers

ASA

Has age done nothing to your eyes? Will there still be that fear, fleeting though it was, when last I saw you? Will that amused, mysterious smile still play upon your lips, despite the fate you brought upon yourself? I can never forgive you for what you took from us—and I will have what is mine. Time is easy for me, as swift and impermanent as death. And what do I want from you now, Caprice, in your new incarnation? I will not know until I touch you.

1

hunter's moon

Smells like old women. Jocelyn sat for a moment, taking it all in, wondering if this gloomy house filled with odors and fear would be the end of her. All her "old women" had lived here: ill-fated great-grandmother Caprice, grandma Nana France, and mother, Constance—Judge Connie to the courtroom minions she ruled.

And just how do old women smell? Constance would have asked in her take-no-crap voice.

Like Chanel No. 5, burned biscuits, Bombay and tonic, Jocelyn replied in her thoughts with a wistful smile.

Never burned a biscuit in my life!

"Come on, Connie!" she said out loud.

"Mom, who you talking to?" asked eleven-year-old Mikela, her eyes wide. She had her father's lashes, so thick they got in her eyes when she blinked, along with his round face and quick grin. As a matter of fact, Mikela was the spitting image of Mike, Jocelyn's ex-husband, despite Constance's insistence that the child looked like her. Unlike gentle Mike, scrappy Mikela loved a good fight, a trait she inherited from her grandmother. She was also strong. Without breaking a sweat, she had helped her mother haul five suitcases filled with clothes, books, and miscellaneous junk into this old house, which was now to be their home. Exhausted, Jocelyn had sunk into the nearest chair.

"Me. I'm talking to me," she answered her daughter.

"Why?"

"Habit."

"That's weird. I don't like it! Don't start going crazy in this creepy old place."

"This house isn't creepy, and don't worry, I'm okay. We both are." *You sure about that?* Mikela's doubtful eyes asked.

"Listen, Miki, we're going to be fine. Grandma isn't here, but she'll always guide and look down on us." *Or up* popped into Jocelyn's mind, and she quickly reprimanded herself.

The "guiding" bit was certainly true. Constance had, for better or worse, been the guiding force in both their lives for as long as either could remember. Despite her objection to Jocelyn's "teenage" marriage, she had supported her through poorly paid stints as a teacher's aide, health food store manager, and lately, part-time assistant librarian. She held Jocelyn's hand in the delivery room when Mike, her "jackass-of-a-husband" (Constance's words), fainted as Mikela squeezed out of her womb. She financed Jocelyn's divorce, scrutinized her friends, and now she was gone, taken at sixty-two, eight months ago, by a fatal heart attack.

"You are breaking my heart, Jocelyn! Shattering it!" Constance exclaimed more times than Jocelyn cared to remember, and here she stood, child in hand, broke-ass as ever, fearing her mother's words were *literally* true. It had taken four months of uncontrollable weeping to finally admit that Constance was gone, and another four to decide to move back home—as good a place as any to grieve. And truth be told, she had nowhere else to go.

Despite her best efforts, and with ongoing shame, Jocelyn knew she had never measured up to her mother's lofty dreams. Both Constance and Nana France were women of consequence in a world that tried to deny them both. Jocelyn followed in no one's footsteps—with the sorry exception of one.

"Just like Caprice! Won't amount to pee!" Nana France wheezed when Jocelyn turned fifteen. "Looks like her, too! Walks, talks like her . . . and that is *not* a compliment, my child!" she added, peering at Jocelyn over red bifocals as she lit her thin black cigar with the sterling silver lighter that was always at hand. She had bought it with her first paycheck, and it was a beautiful thing, heavily embossed with delicate roses. It had fascinated Jocelyn ever since she'd been six and Nana France had let her flick it.

"Caprice?" Jocelyn asked innocently, speaking the rarely spoken name as if she'd never heard it before.

"Capricious Caprice, foolish Caprice. My poor doomed mother!"

"Doomed?" Fifteen and sick of the expectations of hard-driven women, Jocelyn considered "doomed" a romantic thing to be. "What'd she do to doom her?"

Nana France snorted and said nothing.

The story was that Caprice had left her husband and child, then met some mysterious man who used, abused, and tossed her away, condemning her to live her last days in poverty and shame. Clementine, Caprice's ill-tempered sister, had claimed little France (named after the place Caprice dreamed of living), took the child north when her father died, and raised her in Philadelphia with stern eyes and rough hands. Until the day she died, Nana France dipped her head whenever she spoke the woman's name.

"Aunt Clem wasn't a cruel person, just raised during trying times," Constance would explain when Jocelyn asked about the grim-faced woman in the photograph on Nana France's bureau. "Unlike her sister—my grandmother Caprice—Aunt Clem took life seriously."

"But all Caprice did was fall in love!" Jocelyn would say dreamily, intrigued by the subject.

"And abandon her child and life!" Constance answered with a scowl. "And maybe someday you'll understand what an evil, stupid, destructive gesture that was!"

At thirty, the same age as Caprice when she left, Jocelyn now understood. Mikela was older than Nana France had been, but Jocelyn was sure nothing could drive her to commit such a terrible deed. Yet, of what could one really be sure? Jocelyn's life had come undone. All of her dreams, the foolish as well as the noble, had come to nothing. By now, she hoped she'd either be happily married (despite the history of the women in her family) or fulfilling herself in a job that would make her proud of herself and her mother beam. Her goal had been to become a social worker.

Years with critical, occasionally difficult women had given her an empathy with troubled kids, and she had an easy knack for getting them to open their hearts. After college, she'd interned at a school for emotionally disturbed children and quickly became the adult children always sought—like a mother hen spreading her wings, her supervisor teased her. She knew she'd found her calling and did a year of graduate school, but dropped out when she became pregnant with Mikela. She couldn't bring herself to ask Constance for the money to go back. Too much money—with no return—had been given already. Last Mother's Day, when an acquaintance bragged about the luxury spa to which she'd sent her mother, Jocelyn tried hard not to think about her own gifts—the paltry CVS card and drooping pink roses from ShopRite.

As for men? Mike, a sweetheart of a jazz pianist, had been her great love, but their young marriage had gone south as fast as his behind hitting the floor the night Mikela was born. A year ago, she'd fallen wildly in love with Andrew, a stalwart, sharp-witted young lawyer in her mother's old firm. Constance, who usually kept a level head in such matters, was convinced he was the perfect match, the one Jocelyn—and she—had been waiting for. Constance had all but priced wedding caterers when he abruptly stopped calling and returning her calls—breaking Jocelyn's heart, self-confidence, and hopes and making her believe that—yet again—she had let her mother down. To add insult to injury, he had shown up at Constance's funeral sporting a twenty-something with a blond weave bouncing off her tanned, bony shoulders.

But why should she have been surprised? Jocelyn asked herself, when she saw the two of them laughing together. It was common knowledge that the Markham women, pretty and smart as they were, lacked good sense when it came to men; they all seemed plagued by bad luck and worse judgment. Jocelyn's father, an artist with a weakness for vodka, died in a car crash when she was three. Nana France's husband had been a well-respected lawyer before he swindled rich widows out of hard-saved cash. Done with husbands, Constance was outraged when Jocelyn chose to name her daughter after Mike. Thinking of him now, Jocelyn asked Mikela, "So have you heard from your dad?"

"Yeah, I told him we were moving."

"So what did he say?"

"Nothing." Mikela was secretive when it came to conversations with her father. Awkwardly, she changed the subject, avoiding her mother's eyes. "So Ma, what do you think Grandma would say if she knew we were living here now?"

"She'd be glad," Jocelyn said, deciding not to push it.

"She'd probably say, get yourself a plan, huh?"

Jocelyn nodded. "That's exactly what Constance would say."

"Daddy said you shouldn't call Grandma by her first name. It's disrespectful."

"Daddy should mind his own business," Jocelyn said, thinking that if Mike knew what Constance had to say about him, he'd keep his mouth shut. "Here's *our* plan, Miki. First, we'll open some windows in this dusty place and let in some air. Then we'll haul our things upstairs, make our beds, and start putting stuff away. Then we'll order pizza."

Mikela glanced at the ceiling and scowled. "Pizza first."

They studied the take-out menus stacked neatly in a

in the water, poisoned herself with Barbados nut. For love of me, so that I would never leave her. Love has no boundaries, and that was how she proved it; for love of me, she did it. Imagine *that* kind of love."

His words, spilling out as they did—so quick, yet painlessly—made Jocelyn gasp, ashamed that she'd asked him to share something of such horror.

"It was a long time ago," he said with a sidelong glance.

"Oh, my God! I'm . . . I'm so sorry to have made you talk about it. I don't know what to say . . . I. . . ."

He touched her hand, and a spark shot through her that she tried to ignore, embarrassed to feel something so blatantly sexual after he'd shared such tragedy.

"Like I said, it happened a long time ago. And when it did, I thought my life was over, and then I . . . well, I was able to reclaim what I could from it, go on from there."

"But still . . ."

"It was another lifetime," he said. "Believe me."

"But how do you recover from something like that?" The moment she asked, she realized how useless the question was, because she knew the answer before he said it: you didn't.

A darkness settled over him, and the silence between them seemed heavy with dread. Should she leave? Jocelyn wondered. Or apologize for being so intrusive? What in the world had made her ask about such a personal part of his life? But then he turned to her with a tender smile that stirred her.

"I'm sorry to lay it on you like that. I've had a lot of happiness and love since then. My life is what it is."

She understood those eyes now, the melancholy that shadowed them and had struck her so intensely the first time she saw him. Her heart opened to him then as swiftly and earnestly as it did for the lost children who so often gathered under her wings.

Jocelyn waited for a moment, wanting the mood that had settled between them to pass before she spoke again. "And what is that life now?"

His face brightened, as if remembering some pleasure. "I'm a traveler and collector. All over the world, collecting what I need to make me happy. But I've been in love, completely in love, only one time since Marimba. A woman who . . . well, I'd rather not talk about her, but she left me as well, for her own selfish reasons. She's dead now. Unlucky in love, eh?"

"Aren't we all?" Jocelyn said, lifting her glass, glad that the mood had lifted.

"And what about you?" he asked. "Don't start with tragedy. No. Talk about happiness. The thing that makes you smile."

"My daughter," Jocelyn said without hesitation. "There is nothing in my life I treasure more than Mikela." Asa took a sip of champagne, said nothing, and Jocelyn, considering the tragedy that had befallen him, the children he'd lost, wished she'd kept her words to herself. Desperately, she tried to think of something else to add. "I'm sad about my life sometimes," she mumbled, and his eyes turned again to her. "I don't want to end up like . . . well . . . Caprice," she added with a self-conscious chuckle. His shoulders tightened and a hardness came into his eyes. Rising quickly, he stoked the fire, his back toward her.

"And who was she?" His tone was harsh, darker, and Jocelyn, puzzled by the difference, wondered why he reacted as he had. Why had she started all this morbid talk of sorrow and doom? She was getting as bad as Luna. But then he turned toward her, the warmth back in his eyes. "Are you hungry? There's some leftover gumbo that's too much for one."

Jocelyn *was* hungry, and the wine had heightened her hunger. She thought about staying, wondering where things might lead.

"Another night, maybe? No strings attached." He read her uncertainty.

"Yeah. I think so. My ex will be bringing my daughter home later on tonight, and she has school tomorrow." A blatant lie, and she wasn't sure why she told it, except it flowed out with no hesitation. She wasn't a good liar; her face always gave her away. Nana France always warned that even the smallest one etched a tiny mark on one's soul, so it wasn't the lied-to who paid, but the liar. He gave her a quick, curious glance, and she realized he knew it wasn't the truth. It was those eyes again, which could pierce right through her. But he smiled as if he understood.

"Great. It will give me something to look forward to."

She returned his smile, glad to be forgiven. He offered his hand to pull her off the low-slung couch and slightly toward him, but then stepped back, giving her space. She almost wished he hadn't.

"Maybe next weekend? Give me a call if it will work for

you." He handed her an ivory-colored business card with his name and cell number embossed in navy ink.

"Will you make more gumbo?" she asked flirtatiously, surprised how easily flirtation came.

"It's the only thing I can make," he said with a self-conscious half-grin, and she laughed with him, wondering again if she was leaving too soon, but the lie had been told. He walked her to the door and hugged her, lingering just long enough to warm her body before she stepped back into the brisk October air.

5

blood-red roses

Jocelyn couldn't get him out of her mind. She tried hard to hide it, but Mikela knew her too well.

"So what did you do last night?" she asked at breakfast, watching Jocelyn closely as she sipped the last of her coffee. Jocelyn managed a nonchalant shrug.

"Not much."

"So what did you eat for dinner?"

Knowing what she was up to, Jocelyn pointedly ignored her. "Finish your cereal so you can get to school. You don't want to be late again."

"So when did you lose Nana France's earring?"

"What? Oh my God!" Jocelyn grabbed her left ear, feeling desperately for what wasn't there. Could it be somewhere in his house? Maybe she'd lost it on the way over to his place or coming back. It was late when she got ready for bed, and her head swelled with thoughts about him; she'd forgotten she'd had them on. How could she have been so careless? Why hadn't she simply taken the time and money to have the earring fixed? Regret and shame shot through her.

"I thought you said you didn't go out," said Mikela, suspicious.

"Eat your breakfast."

"Did you go out on a date or something?"

Jocelyn glanced at her daughter, wondering if she should tell her the truth—that she'd had a drink with the man next door and had probably lost it at his place—then decided against it. She didn't feel like being cross-examined by an eleven-year-old.

"Wherever I went or didn't go last night—or do or didn't do—is certainly none of *your* business, Miss Thing," she said, using her mother's favorite nickname for Mikela.

Grinning, Mikela finished off her cereal and bit into a piece of toast. "Miss Thing!" she said back playfully.

"Miss Thing back at you!"

"I miss Grandma so much." Mikela grew sad, and the familiar tug of sorrow Jocelyn felt whenever she thought about her mother made her eyes water.

"Me, too," she said quietly.

She wondered again why her mother hadn't mentioned Asa, particularly the business with the cake. Constance, burner of biscuits, was no baker, so she must have bought it somewhere. But it wasn't like her to forget the presence of a rich, handsome, eligible bachelor living next door. Yet it must be the truth; he had no reason to lie.

She glanced at Mikela, who had nibbled the crusts off her toasts leaving behind the buttered middle. She smiled to herself. Most kids hated the crusts. Interesting kid, she had. She'd be an interesting woman someday.

"So did you and your dad have a good time last night?"

"Yeah." Mikela glanced up then back at her plate, unwilling to discuss any of her father's business.

"So what did you do?"

"Not much," Mikela cagily replied. Jocelyn wanted to ask about Gina, the woman Mike had mentioned earlier, but dared not risk it getting back to him.

"So what's your dad's new place like?" That seemed innocent enough.

"Great! It's a two-bedroom. I got my own room."

"No creepy tub?"

"Nope. I want to spend more nights with Daddy."

A pang shot through Jocelyn. "I'll think about it."

"Why?"

"Well, your father works very late at night, and . . ." She paused, then told the truth. "I'd miss you *so* much. And then *I'll* be alone in this house with that creepy old tub like somebody drowned in it."

Mikela giggled and Jocelyn grinned at her mirth. "Not every night, Mom, just sometimes. Like a few times a month or something."

"Sure," Jocelyn said with a forced grin, but the pang was still there.

❧

After she dropped Mikela off at school, she looked around the yard for the lost earring, then shook out her jacket and sweater, hoping it had fallen inside. She thought about calling Asa to ask if he'd found it but decided against it. Better to wait for him to call and mention it then.

Luna agreed with her when they spoke about the matter later that evening. "Don't call him. He would have called by now if he had it, and you don't want him to think you're sweating him."

"I don't think he'd think that. He doesn't strike me as that kind of guy," Jocelyn said defensively.

Luna said nothing, then asked, "By the way, can I keep your great-grandma's papers for a while? I want to go over them again."

"Sure. I haven't had a chance to read my bunch yet. Read them when you get some time." Jocelyn wondered what there was to "go over" but didn't ask. "And about that pendant you lent me."

"Wear it," Luna ordered. Jocelyn shook her head, amused.

When Asa hadn't called by Tuesday, Jocelyn decided that either the Markham women's bad-man-mojo was still going strong—or she should seriously avoid men whose names began with A. Constance had allotted money for "education" in her will. Jocelyn assumed it was for Mikela but then realized it could have been her mother's sly way of hinting she should go back to school. Now was as good a time as any, so over the weekend she began to research graduate schools. Rutgers offered a master's degree in social work that seemed to fit her needs, and she decided to apply for the following September. She still had a lifetime to make her mother proud. It made her feel good just thinking about it.

The next week, Asa sent a bouquet of pink and orange tulips in a white china vase that made her smile and remember spring. She called the number on his business card and left a message thanking him for his gift. Two weeks later, he called, said he'd been out of town and wanted to know if she'd join him for dinner, but it was Parents' Night at Mikela's school, and she never missed that. On Saturday morning he called again. "I won't give up until I get you over here to taste my gumbo, no strings attached," he said in his charming way, and she agreed to come at eight on Saturday night. Mikela had been bugging her about spending another weekend with Mike, and Jocelyn, unwilling to explain a dinner date to a nosy daughter, agreed that this would be a good night for her to go.

Saturday night, Jocelyn sat down across from Asa in his kitchen, which was as bright and simple as the living room was dark and elegant. The walls were sunny yellow and the contemporary white cabinets were broken by black granite countertops and a square cooking island in the center of the room. Everything was perfectly chosen—from the limes piled into a crystal fruit bowl to the burst of sunflowers stuffed into a matching vase on the island.

"You can thank my decorator and housekeeper—not me," he said offhandedly when Jocelyn complimented him on his taste. "I have no decorating sense, so I leave it to the experts. But I can cook gumbo—see, I told you." He lifted the lid off a pot on the stove, and the earthy fragrance of the stew drifted into the room. They drank red wine rather than champagne this time, cabernet sauvignon; she was on her second glass.

"So where did you learn to make gumbo?"

"My mama taught me. All things New Orleans I love."

"So that's where you're from?"

"Yeah. Here and there."

"So what do you do besides buy silver knickknacks, doleful statuettes, and old, deserted houses?" Jocelyn asked, settling comfortably on one of the walnut stools.

He answered between pouring more wine and sliding the gumbo off the gas burner. "I'm a restless spirit who does everything I can to survive."

"Well, that doesn't tell me much! We all do that. More or less. So where do you get your money?" she asked, emboldened by the wine on an empty stomach. He threw her a sidelong glance, and she thought for a moment that she'd crossed a line, but his answer came easily.

"Various ways. I inherited some. My granddaddy was one of those sly New Orleans free men of color who gambled wildly but spent his hard earned money on land instead of women. Probably where I get my love of old houses. My mother was smart. Saved her money. Worked for a white guy who she probably slept with, but he also taught her how to invest. And the rest is none of your business. I'm a lucky man. What can I say?" He added the last with a sly, knowing wink, letting her know she had to accept him at his word. "I've talked about myself, at least what I'm ready to tell at this point, now it's your turn," he said, spooning gumbo, spicy and hot, into their bowls.

It was easy to share bits and pieces of her life. He listened intently, never taking his eyes from hers, as if every word she said was a bond between them. She began with her childhood, revealing amusing details and tidbits about Constance,

Nana France, and finally, even Caprice, between sips of wine and spoonfuls of gumbo.

"You have her spirit," he said.

"Caprice?"

"Yeah."

"That's what they tell me." Jocelyn, chuckling and slightly drunk, was surprised by how unburdened she felt, how completely at ease with this man she barely knew. She thought for a moment about her first date with Andrew. Things had come easily then, too, and she wondered if she was letting her defenses down too quickly. "I'm usually not this frank with people. I'm actually very shy; I didn't mean to babble," she added, embarrassed by her loquacity.

"We knew each other in another life; don't you know that by now?" he said with an amused certainty that puzzled, yet disarmed her.

"Oh, I meant to ask. I think I may have lost an earring when I was here last time."

"The little diamond earring you had on last time? No, I didn't find it, but I wasn't looking." Jocelyn chided herself for not having called him the moment she discovered it was gone, but was touched that he remembered what she'd been wearing. "Maybe it slipped into the couch," he said, and they went into the living room to look.

The bright warmth of the kitchen was replaced by the dark coolness of the living room as they searched among the pillows, underneath the couch and rug, but found nothing. They gave up after ten minutes, and Asa built a fire to chase the chill from the room and offered brandy. Jocelyn wondered if she should take some, then decided a sip or two on a full stomach wouldn't hurt.

She sunk easily into the seductive folds of the couch. She had forgotten how deep and inviting it was, and the warmth from the fire made her languid, and when he kissed her, gently nibbling the soft spot underneath her chin, she was surprised but didn't object. She had, she admitted to herself, imagined that kiss in exactly that spot the first time she saw him.

It had been nearly a year since Jocelyn had been intimate with Andrew, the last man she'd made love to. It had taken her weeks to finally decide to sleep with him, and when she did she had realized just how much she missed sex. It had become a regular thing between them, the getting together on Friday nights in his high-ceilinged, spare apartment; the ordering of Thai or Chinese food; the watching of some Netflix movie on his giant flat-screen TV; and finally making love in his hard, queen-size bed. Their lovemaking had been passionate at first, but then fell into a familiar, predictable pattern that left her bored and wanting. But she was in love with him and quickly forgave his laziness as a lover. She understood now that Andrew's lack of passion had simply been disinterest; he had proven that with his abrupt departure.

Asa's touch brought back everything she'd missed and forgotten about sexual passion. He was filled with ferocity and hunger, and part of her was open to him—mouth, ears, tongue, limbs—and when he stopped—just for a moment—she went limp, desperately wanting to feel him inside her.

"Are you sure about this?" he said. His breath in her ear made her heart quicken, but she pulled away.

"I don't know," she said, remembering Andrew and the disappointment that had followed their relationship. But was Asa really offering a relationship? He'd said "no strings attached" that first night, yet she wasn't ready for that kind of thing either.

"I'll take you places you've never been before," he said half joking. "Look, this thing is up to you. Where we go from tonight. Leave me now if you want to."

"I think I'll stay," Jocelyn said, sure now of the decision she was making, and he kissed her lightly on her lips as he led her upstairs.

His bedroom smelled vaguely of amber sweetened by patchouli, and the sheets were cool and smooth against her skin. When she undressed and crawled in bed beside him, their chill against the heat of his body heightened her senses and pulled her closer to him.

He left no part of her untouched, his lips and fingertips exploring her with an unfaltering knowledge of each piece of her intimate self. When he finally entered her, he gently stroked at first, and then thrust himself so deeply inside she was sure he touched places no one had ever touched before. And for a moment, as lost in his touch and smell as she was, she knew that maybe he was right—they must have known one other in another time and space. How else could he know so much about the secret parts of her that made her scream with pleasure? How else could he know what to whisper in her ear and what would so skillfully bring her to climax? This had never happened before, she told him, when they finally stopped, exhausted and giggling with delight. Not even with Mike, and they had always been good together.

She took in his room as she drifted to sleep—the high soft bed, pale blue walls that nearly matched the sheets and down comforter, the glow from the candles he lit before they made love the second time. She felt at home here, calm and happier than she had been in a long time.

She awoke to the sound of the shower, and when she joined him they made love once more, slippery and comical, enveloped in soft needles of water, almond soap, and the lingering scent of her perfume.

She kissed him good-bye then and went home, still feeling him inside her, and the thought of what they'd done together lingered far into the morning, giving her pleasure whenever she moved. Jocelyn had given herself to him with utter abandon—allowing him liberties with her body that no other man had ever taken.

So when deep-red roses the color of blood arrived at her door Monday morning with the words *next week? same time? same place?* scribbled on a pale blue card, she didn't think twice about her answer.

ASA

I missed your scent, Caprice, your Chanel, the rage in 1925, your perfume. The rich ones drenched themselves in it—the smell floating from the Bentleys that dropped them in Harlem for their nip of Uptown. Yet I could still taste you within her this evening. The touch of your breasts on my body buried me in my past, told me my future when this turmoil is over. She will give me what you would not.

I will have you again, and I will never let you go.

6

his wicked realm

"Hello, my baby," Geneva said, before Luna stepped into the room.

"Mama, how you doing?" As Luna settled on her mother's bed, Geneva turned to gaze out the window beside it.

"Where is it?" she asked.

"Where is what?"

"You know what."

"I loaned it to a friend."

"Get it back." She was wearing the pink robe Luna had brought last time she visited. It hung loosely around her shoulders, emphasizing her fragility. Luna knew her mother was dying. She could smell the faint scent of decay beneath the fragrance of lavender room deodorizer and the stink of urine and unwashed bodies permeating the air. Death was coming; she was certain of that.

But it came with the territory.

This was the best nursing home Luna could find with the little bit of money her father had left. The attendants seemed to change as quickly as she learned their names—

Pearlie, Lucy, Jamal became someone else by the week, but their expressions remained the same, reflecting the considerable woe of their charges. Geneva had lived here for nearly ten years. The walls were the same putrid shade of green and the red linoleum was chipped and dull. Televisions, each turned to a different channel, boomed from each room, interspersed with static from the ancient overhead speakers and rap music blasting from somewhere unseen.

At first, Geneva had been put in a state home for the emotionally disturbed. After her father died, Luna toyed with the idea of letting her mother live with her, then quickly realized that if she were to have a life of her own—one free of the boon and the demands it made on them both—she had to let Geneva go. She convinced the manager of this private hospital that Geneva suffered from nothing more than bouts of delusion and was no danger to anyone nor herself.

But it was private only in the loosest sense of the word, just a few steps above the one run by the state; those steps, however, were crucial ones. She shared the bathroom with only one roommate, an eighty-year-old former nurse, half-blind and suffering from dementia, which Luna considered a blessing for them both. The roommate, Mrs. Charles, was oblivious to Geneva's imaginings, and although she'd been there two months longer than her mother, had generously relinquished the window that looked out on the small garden surrounding the property—a welcome respite from the rest of the place.

"When?" Geneva asked, breaking into Luna's thoughts. She dropped her head, then picked it up, drumming her fingers on the blanket that loosely covered her. "When you give it to her?"

"Last Sunday."

"Get it back!" The tremor that marked her mother's movements was becoming pronounced. How long would she be here? Luna wondered with alarm. Geneva's presence, like the boon she had bequeathed, was both blessing and curse. When she died, Luna knew her loneliness would be insurmountable. Geneva was the only living being she knew who truly understood the gift they shared—and she was her mother, so she loved her dearly. Over the years, she had found it easier to say that she'd "lost" her mother, which in its own way was true. Yet whenever she said it—to Jocelyn, her dead lover, or anyone else—she was overcome with guilt, as if to speak it was to wish it. And she didn't. Not anymore.

Geneva grinned and Luna could feel that grin—toothless as it was—deep within her heart. She grabbed her mother's hand, overcome with the joy that her mother suddenly felt. "Got a glimpse of her," Geneva said. "She pretty, copper-colored, skinny little something."

"Who, Mother?"

"Girl who got the charm. She happy today. Got a child, too, don't she, that girl who got the charm? You was right to give it to her, my baby. If she bother to wear it! Serve her right if she don't." She grunted contemptuously, and Luna marveled at how easily Geneva could swing from warmly loving to nastily vindictive; it took only a thought. It unnerved her when she was younger, but she'd gotten used to it, barely noticing it anymore. Those were the turns of her mother's mind, and she'd learned to accept them.

"Can you help her?"

Geneva's eyes blazed with anger. "That's why you come, ain't it?"

"No," Luna lied, even though she knew it did no good. She'd found that out at three when Geneva slapped her across the room for lying in her thoughts—*thinking* of lying to her was all it took.

"You remember it, don't you, that time I hit you?" Geneva's eyes filled with pain.

"Of course I do," Luna snapped, feeling again the sting of her mother's palm across her face. How long ago had that been? "Children don't forget things like that."

"It was the drink, Luna." Her eyes filled with remorse and tenderness, and for a moment Luna could see her own face in that of her mother. When she'd been a girl, she would run her fingers through her mother's thick reddish hair, which was pressed in those days and would leave the scent of Dixie Peach on her hands.

She would count her freckles and compare them to her own, and slip her fingers into those of her mother, who had always been vain about her hands. They were wrinkled now, an old woman's hands. She would look like this someday, but with no daughter to honor her. "I don't do that no more," Geneva continued. "I can't have it in here, no way. You could bring it to me if—"

Amused, Luna shook her head. "You know better than that."

Mrs. Charles, in the bed across the room, groaned, and Luna went to check on her, touching her head, laying on hands, until the groaning stopped.

"Why you think I want to?" Geneva said from across the room.

"What are you talking about, Mama?" Luna said, even though she knew.

"Why you think I want to help her?"

Luna patted Mrs. Charles's thin hand and gently placed it under her stained blue blanket, then sat back on the end of her mother's bed. She opened her turquoise tote bag and pulled out the packet of papers that Jocelyn had given her the Sunday before.

"Why you think that?"

"Because you owe me that," Luna said with no hesitation, and Geneva smirked.

"Guess I do."

"Will you do something for me, Mama?"

"What, my baby?"

"Will you read these to me like you used to. Just a couple of pages, that's all."

Geneva's face softened, and Luna knew she was remembering all those years ago when Luna had been a child and she and Geneva would squeeze next to each other near the radiator in the place off Bergen. Geneva would read to her then—first from the Bible—Psalms, mostly, and Proverbs and Ecclesiastes—and later things she'd find in newspapers or short snatches of poetry: Langston Hughes, Emily Dickinson, Paul Laurence Dunbar, anything to take her thoughts from those that burned her mind.

Geneva stroked Caprice's papers, running her fingers up the sides and across the words, then poured all her breath into a sigh.

"How this going to help?"

"She left them to the girl with my charm. She wants to tell us something."

"This woman dead."

"I know."

"Why you want me to read them, her heart don't hurt no more."

"So it hurt before?"

"That's what she say. How come you want me to read them?"

"Because I need to know what she says." But it was more than that. When Geneva read, she took on the voice and manner of the writer—be it prophet, poet, prostitute. Her voice often took on a "proper" accent when she read the newspaper, or became resonant and deep with the intonation of a Bible-toting reverend when she recited verses. Movie magazines invariably brought forth the pretentious voice of an actor or actress. When she was a kid, listening to Geneva read was better than watching TV.

It was only when she'd begun to research her mother's family that she learned of Geneva's background, that she was the child of a North Carolina preacher, coddled and loved, despite the boon, and college-educated—only to drop out as a senior after she met Luna's father, gotten pregnant, and left everything she knew behind. Luna often wondered about her long-lost family and who among them shared their gift, and as a child her imaginings had fed her rich fantasy life.

For hours, she would sit and imagine the face of her grandmother or aunt, the voice of an uncle. (Geneva had told

her she had two brothers, one of whom had died as a baby.)
She would draw pictures of how she dreamed her "family
home" would be—so different from the cramped apartments
where the three of them lived. There were always curtains
in the windows and fruit trees thick with apples and pears
in the backyard. When she was a child and would bite into
a crisp apple, she would pretend it had come from her
grandmother's garden, and its juicy deliciousness would
stay with her all day. Flowers, too, grew in that imagined
place: lilacs, daisies, sweet peas, and roses with thorns that
never scratched. She knew that Geneva had gotten her love
of books from her people—Luna's father despised them just
as much as he had everything else to do with his crazy wife.
So she imagined a library filled with sunlight and books—
novels by writers she adored, poetry that touched or stung
her, magazines filled with wonder.

Gazing at her mother, Luna caught a glimpse of that
young woman who perhaps had lived such a life—the round
moon face so like her own now gone slack with age, the
sprinkle of freckles and, above all, the eyes that, despite sickness, sorrow and age, shone bright with curiosity.

"Get my glasses, then!" Luna, the obedient child she had
always been, found the narrow black glasses folded between
layers of toilet paper in the nightstand near the bed and
brought them to her. Geneva began slowly, pausing, then
reading in a sweet, rhythmic voice nothing like her own.

It had been a year—long enough to know the
characters from charlatans and find they were the same,
be they packed in Harlem apartments or shotgun houses

in the dark hills of Virginia. Urged by my landlady, Mrs. Heinz, I was faithful about church and attended each Sunday; my loyal attendance was my undoing. Regina Heinz was kin to Stephanie St. Clair, known throughout Harlem as Madame Queen. They had been girls together in Martinique, and carrying a mended blouse to her on my way to service was what brought me to him.

It was early Sunday morning when Regina asked me to take the well-wrapped parcel to her cousin; it seemed a small service for someone who had shown me such kindness. I wore my Sunday best—secondhand though it was—and touched my neck with Chanel.

I saved the money I earned but occasionally bought some small trinket to remind me of my independence. A wooden box filled with neat linen handkerchiefs embroidered with daises and buttercups was my first gift to myself—and then a bottle of Chanel No. 5 perfume, so popular with the women I served. It had just come out from Coco Chanel in Paris, and everyone was wearing it. It put me on equal footing with those women, and I loved the way it made me feel. It was a taste of glamour that added pleasure to my life. A silly extravagance, perhaps, but an essential one for me.

The morning was bright, though clouds lingered from a midnight storm that rained hail and hammered the roof. Her cousin would be "sorting accounts," as Regina delicately put it, and bade me enter quickly and be on my way, as one never knew what evil lurked in places such as that.

It was a basement cabaret, down four steps to a wooden door that opened with a squeak. The walls were paneled in pine and darkened by shadows, but meager light from the open door flashed brightly on the white linoleum floor that gleamed newly polished. In the front of the room stood a makeshift bandstand, little more than a platform of wide planks, where a piano man, trombone player, and bassist strummed and thumped a loud, brassy tune. "Lady Be Good," I think it was. I'd heard it countless times on the radio. I'm struck by the irony of that song now, but in that moment, its carefree joyfulness made me smile, but my delight was brief. The smell of burnt tobacco and spilled gin lingered in the air and that, mingling with cloying perfume and last night's vomit, made me nauseous. I paused at the door to catch my breath and bearing before entering to search for Madame Queen.

She sat rod-straight at a round table tucked into a far corner. Shredded paper covered it and her rust-colored gown like confetti. Her gold earrings, bold and fanciful, caught the light, and her pitch black hair (dyed, I assumed, because Regina's hair was steel gray) was swept into an elegant upsweep fixed with tiny pearls. She was regal and frightening, and I knew at once why they called her Queen. Two young men sat at her table, their eagerness to do her bidding reflected in their faces.

The music slowed when I stepped into the room, and I knew all eyes were upon me. The place was filled with men of all colors and shapes, chatting and smoking, hunched over the long narrow bar. They were bad men,

I decided, as they saw fit to skip church this Sunday morning. There was still enough of that straight-laced Virginia girl within to make me judgmental. I dropped my eyes as I entered, trying hard not to see them. One of the few women in the place swept past, bumping into me as she headed to Madame Queen's table. She was plump, but pleasingly so, in a cocoa-colored satin dress that fit her snugly. She had a sharp pointed nose and full red lips, and when she bent to whisper in Madame's ear, an overripe breast, the color of apricots, nearly pushed its way onto the table. She gave me a strange glance on her return, head held high, her long, straight-haired ponytail swishing as she walked.

Madame Queen had brought the numbers game to Harlem decades ago, turning many a beggar into a wealthy man, and she was cowed by no one. Her gaze was strong and direct as it fastened on me, hesitating like a frightened child at the door.

"You, girl, come here," she said in her sultry voice, and the music stopped mid-note. Caught in her gaze, I stood transfixed. "You hear me, girl, bring me what you got."

"Yes, ma'am," I uttered, like the girl she'd called me. Swallowed by darkness, I made my way toward her table, praying I wouldn't trip and make a fool of myself. I placed the neatly wrapped package in front of her, careful not to knock over the bottle of rum. I feared yet respected this regal woman. She was my benefactor's cousin, known for both generosity and ruthlessness. She and her friends broke the law at will, and I knew she was capable of anything.

"What's your name?" She put a cigarette to her lips, and it was instantly lit by one of the men. They were twins, or appeared to be at first glance, both the color of ebony with hair coated straight with thick pomade.

"Your name, girl?" I found my voice and told her.

"Caprice," she said with a dismissive chuckle. "Caprice. Humph." Taking a drag on her cigarette, she dramatically blew the smoke in a stream toward the ceiling.

"That gentleman over there, in the middle, he want to meet you, Caprice." She shifted her gaze to the only table besides hers graced with a tablecloth.

He was one of the handsomest men I'd ever seen, with skin as smooth and dark as the dress worn by the woman who took Queen the message and who now sat beside him. Even from where I stood, I could see his dark slanted eyes studying me with undisguised interest. He was tall and well-built; I could tell that even as he leaned back in his chair like he owned the club, which he may have for all I knew. His face was marred by a half-moon scar, but the tiny imperfection only added to his charm, making him less than perfect and somehow more appealing. He wore a sharkskin suit, elegant and conservative. My year's stint at Macy's had taught me to know good clothes at a glance, and this one was well-tailored and not off the rack.

Two men sat beside him blowing smoke rings above their heads like teenagers, and the smoke hovered around them, placing a hazy aura above his head. One man had a hawkish, scarred face, and a wolfish grin that was tight and ugly. The other had a young and thin face with eyes that looked older than he. The woman, who was younger than I thought at first glance, draped herself around the man in the middle and ran her tongue up the side of his neck, a cat claiming her prey. But he was nobody's prey, I was certain of that. He shook her off harshly and she fell back into her seat, a wounded look in her large, sad eyes. Liquor was poured into his glass, but he ignored it, rising he came toward me. I cannot recall my thoughts.

"My name is Ezra," he said.

"Caprice," Madame Queen answered for me. "I didn't know they named colored girls such fancy names like that." He threw her a chilling look, and she sunk into her chair as if she'd been struck. "But it's a pretty name, that one, for a pretty girl," she added, quickly turning back to her accounts.

"Caprice," he said softly, as if he liked the feel of it on his tongue, and hearing him say it, the lilting sensuality of it sent a thrill through me. He reached toward me, took my hand in his, and I felt a stab of pleasure like I'd never known.

"So you live around here, Caprice?"

"Yes," I said, unable to say more.

"Over my cousin's butcher shop," Madame Queen volunteered without looking up.

He smiled as if he knew a secret he was unwilling to share. "Join me at my table, Caprice, and you can have whatever you want. Coffee, tea, champagne? You'll like that." I glanced at the back of the room and noticed

*everyone had gone; the three men and the woman with
the long straight hair were nowhere to be seen.*

*"Go," said Madame Queen, her eyes fixing on me,
and he took my hand and led me away.*

*Months later, as I packed my bag to go and live with
him, Regina Heinz begged me not to leave, solemnly
delivering her cousin's words of warning.*

*"She says she will burn in hell for taking you into his
wicked realm," she said.*

*"But that's silly," I told her. "He loves me and I love
him. Why would she say such a thing?"*

Regina avoided my eyes. "Perhaps, because it is true."

*But it was too late for me to listen; he had me by
then.*

*That night was the first time I tasted champagne—
French, he told me, and as I loved all things French I
was enchanted. I barely remember what we said—only
that I did most of the talking: about leaving the South,
my dreams of becoming a writer, my thoughts of
Harlem . . . and of you. He said very little, only this:
"The moment I saw you I knew you would be mine
forever. And even death, even that, could not part us."*

*It seemed a strange thing to say to a woman one has
just met, yet I felt proud knowing this magnificent man
could want me so much. I took another sip of wine,
sneezing from the bubbles, and he chuckled, clutching
my hand as if I were the most charming creature he'd
ever seen.*

In the months that followed, we went places I'd only dreamed of going: clubs I could never afford, fancy dining rooms, concerts, even the zoo. He courted me as if I were the maiden of his dreams—although he knew about my child and that I was far from maiden. But there was no pressure to fulfill that part of our love, although with each touch I wanted to give myself in the only way a woman can truly give herself to a man. Marriage was what I dreamed of. A divorce from Franklin and all the ill he brought me. A way out of this life and a means to bring you back to me. And he promised me that I could—bring you up to live with me again. If only for a while. But it was only in the end that I knew what the cost of that would be.

One evening we sat in the bedroom of one of the older, more beautiful brownstones he owned in Harlem. It sat on Sugar Hill—they called it that then, and sweet it was. It was an enormous house, four stories tall, but he lived only on the first two floors. I'd always admired these stately homes and only imagined how they might look like inside. But I quickly grew used to this one—the elaborate iron gate leading to a front door decked with gas lanterns, the long, narrow windows and crystal chandeliers that lit each room in shimmering light. Everything within hinted at enormous wealth, yet I never asked him how he made his money. He was secretive about that kind of thing, and I didn't want to annoy him with probing questions. I was sad that day. I'd hoped a story I'd submitted would be published in a journal of work by new Negro writers, and it had been rejected. He tried to cheer me.

"What else do you need but me?" he said, and I smiled at his assumption. But I had begun to wonder myself. He kissed me as he always did, with tender reverence, and then his kisses grew stronger, more passionate, and I was caught in his fervor. That night he claimed me wholly, body and soul, and everything between us changed forever. But there was no talk of marriage.

Weeks later, I awakened to his gaze, frightened by its intensity. I kissed him gently, hoping to soften those dark, brooding eyes, and he returned my kiss, fiercely, biting and bruising my lips.

"You will never leave me," he muttered, and I thought, perhaps, this was his coy way of asking me to marry, but he quickly relieved me of that fantasy when he abruptly rose from our bed.

"But why?" His words left me at a loss. It was raining that day, and I dreaded leaving the warmth of our bed to head downtown. I pulled him to me, searching for an answer, and when he spoke there was an expression in his eyes that frightened me. "You can share it with me, my love," I said.

"Are you ready for my truth?"

I nodded because I thought nothing he could tell would be more than I could bear. For the more he possessed my body, the more of my soul was lost.

Geneva finished reading, rocking as if the reading had taken something from her, and Luna watched her mother, said nothing, sensed what her mother felt because the dead woman's words had touched her, as well. Caprice's spirit had filled them both, and neither could speak.

"Mama," Luna finally said, breaking the spell upon them. "Mama!" Geneva looked up, her eyes empty, as they often were when the boon was in control. "Mama, come back!"

"I haven't gone anywhere, at least not where he can find me." Luna gasped at Caprice's voice still coming from her mother's lips. She grabbed Geneva, shook her hard.

"Let her go! Come back, Mama, I need you." Geneva fell back into the pillow, eyes aglow as she studied her daughter's face.

"Ain't gone nowhere," she said and Luna smiled at the sound of the familiar voice. She filled a plastic pitcher on the night table with water from the sink in the front of the room and poured some into a Styrofoam cup. Geneva grabbed it, gulping eagerly, spilling most of the water down her chest.

"Who was she talking about?" Luna asked. Geneva said nothing. "You know, don't you, Mama, you got to tell me."

"Stay away from him."

"He means to hurt my friend."

"The one with your charm? She gonna need it, baby."

"What is his truth?"

"Just like the lady say. He one of them that take your soul."

"And who is 'them'?"

Geneva smiled and shook her head. "Don't you know by now?"

"What is he, Mama, man or demon? Is he . . . alive?"

Geneva nodded. "But he got to eat your soul to stay that way, same as beast need flesh. They come in patterns to get their fix. Just like a junkie. You got to give it up for him to claim it. You got to die for him to get it."

"And what if you don't give it?"

Silent, Geneva closed her eyes, telling her daughter there was nothing more she knew or cared to say.

7

unconscious beauty

Jocelyn saw him the next weekend and, after that, all the ones that followed. She'd make Mikela breakfast, wait for her to catch the bus, and if Asa was at home, climb into his bed, careful to be home before Mikela returned. Mikela stayed with Mike most weekends, and at first she was glad to be spending so much time with her father, but by November, Mikela had grown watchful and suspicious, and Jocelyn knew she would soon have to tell her how deeply involved she was with Asa. She wasn't looking forward to it. How could she explain such exquisite pleasure to an eleven-year-old? But there was no avoiding it.

"So, Mom, tell me about this guy you're going out with," Mikela said one Monday morning as she settled down on the edge of Jocelyn's bed. She had just finished her cereal and was getting ready to go to school. Jocelyn wondered if she could tell the bed hadn't been slept in. "Were you with him last night?"

"Asa. I told you his name is Asa," Jocelyn said patiently, sure she had told her at least twice, but perhaps she hadn't.

The more time she spent with Asa, the more she couldn't remember what she'd told or not told her daughter. Her days away from him seemed blurred and dull. It seemed as if she forgot everything: the lyrics to songs she'd sung all her life, the titles of books she'd read twice. She'd stick milk into cabinets and empty bowls into the refrigerator—like some poor soul with dementia, she thought. It frightened her, this forgetfulness, but then she decided that his presence in her life overshadowed everything else. "And . . . as far as your other question goes, you're old enough to understand there are certain things you don't ask your parents, and that's one of them. It's none of your business, sweetheart."

"It is my business because you're my mom." Tears filled Mikela's eyes, and Jocelyn felt her own begin to water. Constance always teased her about being too tender when it came to her child, and maybe she'd been right. Mikela's tears always softened her heart.

"Asa and I are friends. More than friends." Jocelyn hoped that would be enough.

"Do you know what those roses mean?"

"The roses Asa sent me?"

"What else?"

"No, Mikela, I don't." Jocelyn settled beside her daughter on the bed, wondering if now was the time to share how close she and Asa had become, but a glance at Mikela's face told her otherwise. She had to find a way to bring the two together. Problem was, Asa seemed as unwilling to meet Mikela as she was him. She suspected it was because of the loss of his own children, and that thought reminded her to tread gently.

"Unconscious beauty. That's what those roses he sends you mean. Yellow roses mean friendship. Remember Daddy gave you those? White mean innocence. But dark red roses like the ones he sends, roses that look like gore, mean unconscious beauty. That's weird that he sends you something that means 'unconscious beauty.' Like you don't know you're pretty. What kind of dumb thing is that to say to somebody?"

Unconscious beauty. Jocelyn smiled despite herself. Did he know her better than she knew herself? She always felt slightly somnolent when she was with him, as if she were in a dream world. Was that a bad thing? She'd never felt beautiful before. Pretty sometimes, cute when she'd been a kid, but never gorgeous in the way he told her she was. The way he touched, gazed, kissed made her feel lovely and adored. She'd been so scared she'd end up bitter and mistrustful, like her mother could often seem, but she was learning to trust again, to accept the dream for what it was, and she was grateful to him for that.

"Hurry up so you won't miss the bus," she said to Mikela.

"So you can get back to him?" Mikela tossed it out, staring defiantly. Jocelyn took a deep breath, tried to regain her composure

"I don't feel like this mess this morning," she muttered. "Listen, Miki, I love you. Nobody will ever take your place. There's no need to be . . ."

"You think I'm jealous . . . of him?"

"I'm just saying there's no need for you to be."

"You're not going to do something dumb like marry that creep, are you?"

"He's not a creep," Jocelyn snapped.

"So why aren't you going to the library every week like you used to? You used to like to go there. So you can spend more time with him, Mr. Rich-Ass, Silver Car?" Mikela was baiting her; Jocelyn tried hard not to bite.

Taking a deep breath, she said, "I'm not going to the library every week because I want to go back to graduate school in September and I need the time to prepare, to study for the GREs and a few other tests I need to take." That was a blatant lie. She'd stopped thinking about grad school weeks ago. It had been Asa's idea for her to work every other week; it had nothing to do with grad school. He would give her the extra cash if she needed it, he said, and they could have more time together. She resisted at first, wondering if it fed into some need to be taken care of, but he kept at her about it and finally she gave in.

"You're lying, Mom. Where are your books if you're really thinking about grad school? Where's the stuff you're supposed to be studying?"

Jocelyn stood up, hand raised as if to strike her daughter, then brought it back down to her side. Where had that violent impulse come from? She had never raised her hand at her daughter before.

"I told you, I need time to prepare for the GREs," she said, softening her voice, avoiding her daughter's eyes, but she was frightened by how quickly the anger had come, how easily the lie had slipped out. Yet she had begun to realize that the more she lied the easier it became. She answered Luna's texts with lies, telling her how Asa meant nothing, how they rarely saw one another. She lied to Mike about small things, for no reason. The only person she couldn't lie to was Asa, who looked through her and saw everything she was afraid to say.

She reached toward Mikela, trying to embrace her, but Mikela turned away and ran downstairs and out of the house, slamming the front door behind her. Jocelyn stood at the window and watched her waiting for the bus, telling herself she would make it up to her at dinner. And that evening she tried to.

"Listen, Miki, I'm so sorry about this morning, I—" she began.

Mikela interrupted her. "I want to stay with Daddy during the week and you on weekends."

Jocelyn poured herself a third glass of wine. It was one of the vintage ones, from the case Asa had brought her back from somewhere. "When you taste these wines, think of me tasting you," he told her, and when she drank she thought of him; it made it easier to cope until she saw him again on Fridays.

"No," she said to Mikela. "I want you here with me."

"Why? You act like I'm not here. Like you don't even see me."

"How could I not see you when you're sitting in front of me?" Jocelyn joked; Mikela stared back stone-faced. "You think if you're here on weekends, I won't see Asa. That won't work, Mikela, he's in my life now."

"You drink too much wine, Mom. You never did before. You act like a fucking drunk!"

"Mikela, don't say words like . . ." But it was too late. Mikela had dramatically left the room.

"The hell with it," Jocelyn muttered, taking another sip

of wine. It seemed that every time she tried to make peace with her daughter, the wrong words tumbled out of her mouth. At this point, it didn't seem worth the bother.

❧

"I want to take you somewhere special," Asa said the weekend before Thanksgiving. "Maybe two places. Or three. I'm telling you ahead of time so you can do something with the kid."

"The kid has a name," Jocelyn reminded him, passing the joint they were sharing. She'd rarely smoked before she knew him. Occasionally, she'd take a toke at parties to fit in, and that was it. Despite the claims of her friends that marijuana brought insight and clarity, it had done nothing for her but give her a headache.

It was different with Asa. Smoking weed had become an essential part of their lovemaking, of their connection, and when she could feel him inside her, his fingers running over every bit of her body, she felt alive and craved it more.

"Maybe your ex will keep her for the week. Let you have her on weekends. Do that for me, baby." He kissed her breast, holding her nipple hard and fast between his lips.

She flinched. "That hurts."

"But you like it," he said, and it was true. He could make her swoon with pleasure, turn it into pain, and then switch it back again before she knew it was over.

"I want to take you to Vegas," he said. "We'll give thanks for that."

So she asked Mike if he would take Mikela during that week.

"Please, Daddy, please," Mikela, listening from the other room, yelled out. "Let me live with you during the week." Mike glanced at Jocelyn curiously, hesitated, then he nodded that it was okay, and something broke in her heart when he agreed.

❧

In the weeks she didn't work, Jocelyn traveled with Asa wherever he went. They were spur-of-the-moment, frenzied trips to Los Angeles, South Beach, and Atlantic City, where she was swallowed up in the private clubs, dim and sordid, that he liked to frequent. Sometimes, they'd take a quick flight to Montego Bay—down and back the same day—just long enough for her to sit by the ocean for few blessed moments and try to catch her breath, be calmed by the music of the sea, before they'd hit the clubs with their driving rhythm and wary locals who eyed them both suspiciously. Children in particular were afraid of him—selling their handmade wares or asking for money. One look and they would flee.

She remembered one child in particular, a boy of about ten, who had tried to sell them trinkets on the beach of their hotel. Handsome kid, big eyes, bigger smile. He had a rhythmic accent so charming it made her want to buy everything he sold. Unlike the others, he'd stayed, begging the "pretty lady" to buy his wares. Asa was tired that morning. A night of drugs and drink had left him surly and impatient. Leave us alone, he'd told the child, but the boy ignored him, fixing his eyes on Jocelyn. Asa beckoned him close, as if ready to buy something, then grabbed the child's wrist instead, squeezing and twisting until he yelped in pain. Terrified, the boy ran away. Jocelyn took all the money she had in her bag and chased him down the beach. When she caught him, she tried to stuff dollars and euros into his hands, but he wouldn't touch them; he wouldn't even look at her.

"Why did you do that to him, you son of a bitch?" she screamed at Asa when she returned. But Asa said nothing. Finishing his drink he'd simply watched the sun begin to set in the distance.

He knew people everywhere, it seemed—silent and morose when first greeted but quickly brought to life with the liquor and coke he offered freely. She never asked the names of his friends, and he never told her. It was easier to keep quiet, enjoy the safety of ignorance, of his presence in places where she knew no one. Wasn't this one of the dreams she'd always had? she reminded herself. To go places she'd never been?

She'd been embarrassed at first—by the way he spent money so freely—showing off, it seemed—sharing drugs he got from, she wasn't sure where, throwing cash away on her or wild-eyed women she didn't know. He'd leave with them some nights, yet always returned to her in the morning.

And it was fun going to warm places in the middle of the winter when everyone else was bundled tight and sleeping under comforters. He made her feel confident, beautiful in a way she never had before. There had always been a streak of puritanism in the cores of the Markham women. They spent their money frugally, rarely on clothes or extravagant jewelry. A wanton love of luxury was something both Nana France and Constance frowned upon, so Jocelyn had never allowed herself to have it. Asa made her feel differently.

"You deserve beautiful things. Let me give them to you," he would say when she seemed unsure about the gifts he would bestow—the emerald earrings, a rope of pearls. "Are you afraid of who you are, who you are destined to become?"

"The original me?" she asked once, half-joking, remembering what she'd said to Luna that night.

"Original?" he scoffed. "Nobody is original. I've seen you before."

"You think so?" she said, annoyed.

"Well, if original is what you want to call yourself, it's fine with me," he said with some disdain.

She began to enjoy letting him buy things she would never have worn at home—skintight satin sheaths that slipped over her slender body and appealed to other men in ways that made her uncomfortable at first. Then she grew to enjoy the attention—from them and from him. And when she wore the ones that dipped deep down her naked back, she liked the way he ran his fingers down her body into the crack of her ass—claiming her as his property.

As it grew colder, they traveled to the Caribbean more. She drank so much rum the smell of rum cake turned her stomach.

"Do you trust me," he would ask each night before they went to bed. "Do you trust me to always keep you safe?"

"Yes, I do," she would tell him again and again, until she believed it herself.

"I want to try different things," he asked before they left for Negril the day before Christmas.

"Like what?"

"Something you'll like," he said, and she told him yes, because she knew he wanted to hear it.

So on Christmas Eve, he shared her with a guy he said he'd known for years—someone safe for this first experience. Ugly man, mean-spirited, but she had told Asa she trusted him, so she went along with it. The feel of the man's fingers, rough and dirty, roaming her body, digging into her. His smell like death, and Asa taking it all in, savoring it with pleasure. When she remembered snatches of it later, she wasn't even sure when or where they had been. All she remembered was the bed—red sheets, wide enough for four. Who had been the fourth? Some woman grabbed from somewhere. What had they all done together? She didn't remember nor care, except the woman smelled better than the man—like the sea, she thought. But she knew it was Christmas morning because carolers were singing. She wept when they sang "Joy to the World," Nana France's favorite carol.

"Stop it!" Asa told her, smacking her hard across the face. "Don't embarrass me." And she did. He'd only slapped her once, she reminded herself, and he promised he'd never do it again.

Another time, another city, they wore blindfolds—more

mystery and fun, he'd said—and she'd found a strand of long, straight hair on the pillow the next morning and re-called a glimpse of apricot-colored skin barely covered by the sheets when she'd stumbled out of bed at dawn to use the bathroom. Man or woman—she didn't ask, nor about the scar on her wrist where she'd been bound. It cut deep and didn't heal for days. She'd been too high to care.

✂

Somehow she made normalcy return on Friday when Mike brought Mikela home. She would watch Asa as he pulled out after she left on Friday mornings, and listen for him on Sundays, never awake when he returned. On some Fridays, she would be coming in through the back door just as Mike rang the front doorbell, and she'd open the door avoiding her daughter's angry, curious eyes.

In January, she noticed Mike's furtive glances around her house, his obvious disgust as he walked through each un-kempt and dirty room. One morning, she allowed herself to view her home as he did and was shocked by what she saw: crusty dishes piled up on counters flanked by filmy glasses; soiled, empty cartons from Chinese restaurants and pizze-rias; unread newspapers piled high against the wall. She'd closed her eyes; she had no time to clean. There was no time to wash dishes or scrub counters or put things in the washer or dryer. Her traveling with Asa left her exhausted on the weekends, so she lay in bed missing him beside her, making forced conversation with her sullen daughter. They'd order pizza for dinner, eat in front of the TV set, and have cereal for breakfast. Mikela watched her, saying nothing, pouting and picking a fight whenever she could.

And then began the nightmares.

8

a pawing at my heart

"So tell me about that nightmare you have when we're not together," Asa said to Jocelyn as they made love on a Friday morning in February. She straddled him, riding long and hard, feeling him so deeply inside her she couldn't think. He nipped at her breasts, missed, and she giggled amid strides as he brought her down to him, licking the tender space between her breasts, then nicking the spot on her neck that thrilled her.

"What?" she screamed, dizzy with pleasure.

"Tell me," he said, losing his breath as they climaxed, and she tumbled beside him, gasping for air.

"My God! What kind of thing is that to ask somebody doing *this*!"

"I want to know, that's all. About that nightmare that scares you. Keep dreaming it if it brings you to me every day and night."

"Not *every* day and night," Jocelyn said. "I *do* go home on weekends."

"So tell me," he asked as she snuggled next to him, taking

his breath into hers, feeling his body against her. The memory of the dream made her shiver—it was the dread that came with it, more than anything else, the deep, encompassing dread. It began with foreboding. She would open her eyes, unable to move. Lying still in the thick darkness, she could feel an indescribable presence settling on her chest and pawing at her heart, hoping to enter it, and she was consumed by fear. Was she asleep or awake? She wasn't sure until sunlight flooded the room. There were no words to describe her terror.

"Well, I'm lying in my bed . . ."

"Without me next to you, that's the first problem." She touched his lips with her fingertips, urging him to listen.

"And like this terrible sense of fear comes over me, then there's something on top of me, trying to scratch its way into my body."

"Maybe it's me. But I don't scratch!" he said, which was a lie. He had covered her once with goat's blood and scratched it off, painting pictures like henna tattoos on her back and breasts.

"But I know something horrendous will happen if I don't let it in, but I can't. I'm too afraid. Maybe it's some kind of a warning."

"A warning? Why? What do you need to be warned about? So then what happens?"

"I wake up and the sun is up, and I wait for the weekend to be over so I can be with you again."

She lay still as he sprinkled cocaine on her belly and snorted it off greedily. She'd never done coke before she met him, and he never missed a chance to tease her about it.

What? Married to a jazz musician and never done blow? Truth was, Mike was the straightest musician she knew. Too many bad stories, Mike said. His music was enough to get him high; the most he drank were Bud Lights.

Heroin was an interesting high, too, Asa told her, close enough to death to make you curious. She'd done it with him twice and gone into a nod, her head rocking back and forth into nothingness, which felt like death until she threw up, violently, her stomach in knots. The newest one was meth; he said, let's do that, but she'd seen too many photographs of women with no teeth and wouldn't try it. She was too afraid of death, and that made her afraid of life, he claimed, which annoyed her, but not to the point that she let him know it. But a couple lines of coke felt good some mornings. It was his favorite way to start the day—makes me want to fuck you till you die, he would say when they did it, and that scared her at first, but then he would lose interest in sex altogether, pace the floor, snort what he could until there was no more. It was different for her. The drug made her confident, energetic, superior even to him.

It was a dreary morning, and the rhythm of the rain beating on the skylight made her edgy. This was her week at the library and her shift started at noon, but she didn't feel like going. At Asa's suggestion, she'd called in sick the week before last, and if she wanted to keep her job, part-time though it was, calling in again was out of the question.

"So that's the end of the dream?" He started the conversation up again. "You lying there being scared."

"Yeah, except it stays with me, that's all."

"So what do you think it means?"

Jocelyn shrugged. "I have no idea, except I only have it when I sleep at home."

"So are you one of those psychic bitches, who knows the future and shit? So what do you dream about when you're here?" He avoided her eyes. Jocelyn wondered why but didn't ask. She never questioned that faraway look that came unbidden into his eyes.

"Nothing. The minute after we do our thing and my head hits the pillow, I'm out, like I'm drugged."

Chuckling, Asa took a long drag off a joint, pulling it in long and easy, reminding Jocelyn of the first time she saw him, and she felt the familiar warm tug in the pit of her belly. "Got news for you, baby, you are. Feels good, don't it."

Unconscious beauty.

"You're incorrigible," she said, shaking her head.

"You don't know the half."

They showered together, moved into the kitchen, sipped mimosas then coffee, ate buttered toast and an omelet made of mushrooms, onions, and red peppers, of which he fed her forkfuls, even though she wasn't hungry, and when bits of onion dropped into her lap, he nibbled them off, tickling her with his tongue, sending them both into gales of laughter as they rolled onto the cool of the kitchen floor. It was nearly noon before she made her way back into the bedroom to get dressed for work.

"So why don't you . . ."

"Don't say it. I can't call in sick again."

"No. Quit. There's no reason for you to go in at all. We could go all kinds of places. Far away. Leave everything behind and belong to me completely. Let him have the kid until we need her again. Leave her until then. What else do you need?"

"I'm not ready yet." She hadn't realized she'd said it until the words tumbled out of her mouth; she wondered where they came from.

"Then when?" His irritation startled her. Her cell phone rang on the night table; she turned it off.

"So who was that? Besides somebody you don't want to talk to."

"My friend. Luna." *Friend.* Saying Luna's name again, thinking about her as a friend, brought a strange sense of calm, one she hadn't felt in months.

"Luna?" He looked interested. "What does she want?" Jocelyn had told him enough about her to make him suspicious.

"She doesn't trust you."

"Why?" he said with feigned innocence.

"I'm not sure." Jocelyn was unwilling to repeat Luna's half-baked theories about the "evil" Asa brought. Maybe in Luna's world of mystical thoughts and spiritual transformation, much of what they had done in past months would be considered evil, but she had grown in many directions— experienced life in ways that she never thought she could. There was nothing inherently evil about that, she was just different from whom she had been. She'd done things with him—for him—that she'd never done before. Wasn't that growing? Experiencing life in new and diverse ways?

"Come on, tell me. You two are best friends, right? Isn't that what you used to say? Look at me!" he grabbed Jocelyn's chin and forced her to face him. He was doing that

more often these days, when she wouldn't tell him something he wanted to know, and she didn't like it. She snatched
her head away.

"Okay then, I'll tell you. She said you would bring evil
into my life."

"Evil? What the fuck is that?"

"What you are, according to Luna."

"She must be some silly kind of bitch to be throwing
around that shit. She doesn't even know me. Sometimes you
need to cut folks out, baby, not give them the ropes to your
life or they'll strangle you with their stupid beliefs. Evil is
just like God, an outdated concept. Come here," he said,
pulling her to him.

"No, not now," Jocelyn said, avoiding his embrace, suddenly uncomfortable. She gave him a peck on the lips.

"Where you going?"

"Work."

"We'll finish this on Monday," he yelled at her as she left
the kitchen through the back door, slamming it behind her.

The cold wind slapped her hard in the face when she
stepped outside. Away from him, she came back to herself
as icy rain pelted her. She remembered that she'd promised
to show Laura, the head librarian at her job, a copy of Caprice's papers, and she headed into the house to get them.
Luna's call had made her remember.

In late January, she'd listened to Luna's messages and
read a few of her texts—dire warnings urging her to read
the papers her great-grandmother had left, ominous predic-
tions about what would befall her if she continued to spend
time with Asa—words more like the rants of a crazy woman

than the Luna she knew. Jocelyn had begun to wonder if she was passing down the same path as her mother.

She could go weeks without thinking about Luna, then a whiff of ginger, a glance at the moon, would bring her back. The week before Christmas, before the trip to Jamaica, Luna had surprised her outside the library. They'd hugged like the old friends they were, and Jocelyn, wrapped in her friend's embrace, realized just how much she missed her. But then Luna had started in about Asa, how he wasn't all he seemed, how there was something that she must be made aware of, that he wasn't a man like most men, he was evil and she must leave while she still could. Disgusted, Jocelyn had pulled away enraged.

"If that's all you have to say, then we have nothing to say," she'd told her.

"Jocelyn . . ."

"No. Enough. Nothing, not even you, will ruin this for me! He's taken me places, showed me worlds that you could never understand."

"Places you'd never go on your own," Luna said with a nasty edge.

"Places you'll never go!" she snapped, regretting the meanness of the words the moment they left her mouth, but it was too late to call them back.

Remembering those last words, Jocelyn wished she hadn't been so harsh. If Luna was on the verge of some kind of breakdown, wasn't this the time to listen to her and offer support? Feeling petty and ashamed, she dialed Luna's number, smiling at the sound of the familiar voice on the answering machine.

"Hey Luna, sorry I haven't been in touch . . . uh, give me a call when you get a chance. You know I love you!" she added. She meant that, if not the rest of it. But at least she had reached out to her. At least . . . nothing. She sighed tucking her phone back into her bag.

When she entered her house, the stink overwhelmed her. She'd forgotten to take out the garbage last weekend and opened cans of rancid food overflowed the trash can. Milk Mikela had spilled still sat, sour and sticky, on the counter. She'd been in such a rush to get to Asa she hadn't stopped to wipe it up. Coffee-stained cups filled with dregs of coffee were in the sink, along with plates filthy with dried egg and leftover bacon.

But she had to get to work. There would be time to clean before Mike dropped Mikela off tonight; she'd do it then. She heard Asa's car back out of the driveway at breakneck speed, and she wondered for a moment where he was going. When she was with him, she couldn't bring herself to ask him, yet she wanted to know. Could he be spending his weekends with some other woman? One of those who left with him for his moments of "privacy" in Atlantic City? She'd never questioned him.

You never knew what men were really up to. They could make wild frantic love to you in the morning, and be doing something with somebody else before the sun went down. She assumed it had something to do with business, but she didn't know much about that either, except what he'd told her. Men were funny about that, too. Standing in the kitchen, she could almost hear Nana France's advice on men and money: Don't trust a man who won't tell you where he's going. Don't trust a a man who won't say where he gets his cash.

"Oh my God," she said aloud as thoughts about Nana France and Constance among the creaks and sounds of the house hit her so hard she had to sit down.

"Well, that was your experience, Nana France," she said aloud, as if her grandmother were in the room, "considering what my grandfather put you through. It's different for me!"

Don't be so sure!

"Leave me alone!" Jocelyn muttered, just like she used to when she'd been a teenager, as she headed up the stairs to find Caprice's papers. She'd meant to do some washing—for weeks she'd meant to—but black plastic bags of dirty clothes nearly blocked her way into her bedroom. Yet when she opened the bedroom door, the scent of Chanel hit her stronger than usual.

Where was it coming from? Always eager for memories of Constance, Mikela must have spilled some last weekend, then been too embarrassed to confess. She smiled at the thought of her daughter's mischief. Suddenly the thought of Mikela brought an ache of unbearable sweetness to the center of her heart, and she sat down, overwhelmed by it. What were the last words Mikela had spoken, so filled with anger and resentment? What had she said back? How had it come to this? Funny how missing Mikela came on her so suddenly, out of nowhere. She could do with a whiff of Constance, herself; she opened a bottle and brought it to her nose.

"I miss you so much, would you be happy for me now?" she said to the empty room as she lay down for a moment on the unmade bed, pulling the comforter up to her chin, enveloping herself in cozy well-being. Would the nightmare come back in daytime, that terrible dread? But she felt nothing save the soft warmth of the worn comforter.

Her cell phone rang from the kitchen where it lay on the table. Luna, no doubt. She'd give her a call at work, she decided, as she slipped on her work clothes and collected Caprice's papers. Tossing them into a white trash bag so they wouldn't get wet, she headed out the back door.

9

too deep for healing

The rain had turned to hail by the time Jocelyn got to the library. Laura, her boss, sat at her computer, eyes glued to the screen. She was a tall, thin woman in her early fifties with hair that changed color by the season. It was dark brown now, nearly the same shade of her flawless skin, but it would be lightened in the spring; by August, it would be the color of wheat. Laura had a friendly laugh that bubbled just underneath her smoky voice and always set Jocelyn at ease, no matter how sad she was feeling. She needed a boost today. She didn't like to quarrel with Asa, and the irritation in his voice troubled her. His anger had come from nowhere and frightened her. Sometimes, it was as if someone she didn't know had taken him over, even though he always returned to himself—the person she was sure she loved. But didn't everyone have that duality? Didn't she?

Jocelyn turned her attention to Laura, noting with pleasure that she was sipping tea from the red and green mug she'd given her for Christmas.

"Thought you said you were coming in late today? I

wouldn't blame you if you had, in all this rain," Laura said with an exaggerated shudder. The room was a welcome respite, its orange and yellow walls nearly covered by a whimsical mural of *The Cat in the Hat* drawn by ambitious sixth graders. It brought light and humor into a tight working space, making it cozy and comfortable. The scent of coffee and cinnamon cookies, probably brought by one of the volunteers from the senior center, drifted in from the small kitchen, and the smell made Jocelyn feel composed and content, as if she had escaped into a sanctuary.

"Did I say that?" She must have forgotten. "Well, it's nice to be here, even on a day like this." Especially on a day like this, she thought.

She felt at ease here, safe from the swings of emotions that afflicted her when she was alone and glad again that she still had this job, thankful that Laura allowed her to keep such strange hours. Laura claimed it worked out fine; the library had to make budget cuts and Jocelyn's biweekly part-time schedule allowed her to keep others working. Jocelyn suspected it would have been cheaper to simply eliminate her spot altogether, so she was grateful.

She sat down at the desk across from Laura, who glanced up and smiled. "Don't forget to bring in that manuscript from your grandmother. We could do a great display on unpublished black women writing during the Harlem Renaissance. We're too late for Black History Month, but we can do it late in March for Women's Month."

"Brought it in today," Jocelyn said, holding up the parcel.

"Plastic garbage bag!" Laura shook her head disapprovingly. "It deserves better treatment than that, Jos."

"I know, but I thought I was running late, and I wanted to keep the pages dry."

"But still . . ."

"There's just so much crap going on in my life, Laura, I grabbed the first thing I could find."

"It be's that way sometimes," Laura said, nodding as if she understood as she turned back to her work. That was another thing Jocelyn appreciated about her boss; she never asked about the "crap" going on in her life.

"I'm going to go through them again, if that's okay."

"That's fine. Oh, by the way, how's that application for grad school going. Did you get it in yet?"

She must have lied to Laura, too.

"Still working on it," Jocelyn mumbled.

"Well, if you don't go in September, try for January. But do get your great-grandma's papers to me as soon as you can so I can put in for some money to advertise it in the paper."

"Will do."

"I'm going to get some lunch from across the street, want me to bring you something?" Laura grabbed her rain-coat from the closet.

"That's okay. Had a late breakfast."

Jocelyn clicked on her computer and smiled at her screen saver. It was a photograph of Mikela taken in the summer. Sunlight beamed around her, shining on her grin and eyes wide with happiness. A wave of sorrow passed over her. How long had it been since she had seen her daughter smile? Sad and ashamed, she quickly Googled Rutgers University School of Social Work and then the University of Phoenix.

Maybe she could do it, still try for September. For a moment, she imagined herself back in school, talking with troubled kids, actually doing what she had told everyone she was going to do. There were several universities close to where she lived and some had programs she could do part-time. She could make time to do that.

Then she remembered Asa. After vaguely mentioning grad school early in their relationship, she'd never spoken of it again. Each day he seemed to demand more—mind and body—and she always gave it. He needed her as nobody else ever had. Where would *he* fit in all this? What about the traveling they did? Would he find someone else? God knew, there were enough single women out there. He wouldn't have any trouble hooking up with whoever caught his fancy. Maybe now wasn't the time to go back.

Clicking on her directory, she began reviewing library schedules at the various branches. Bored doing that, she opened the bag with Caprice's papers and pulled out a page to read. If she read a few pages now, she could go through the rest tonight at home. Then they'd have an idea how to advertise the manuscript—and if there was enough information to warrant an exhibition. She was having second thoughts about sharing Caprice's observations about the cruelty of her first husband—family secrets, Nana France would have said with a scowl. Maybe she could find something appropriate that would put Caprice and the rest of the family in a good light.

This page, however, wasn't it. There was only a paragraph written in large bold script.

*I will die before I let him have me. I will die before I
let him have me. I will not let him have me. For he is a
lie and all he has ever been is a lie. All has been a lie.
All of it! He cannot have me.*

"Oh lord!" Jocelyn said out loud.

"Things aren't that bad, are they?" Laura said, coming
back into the office, dripping wet and holding a wet paper
bag. She took off her coat, shook off some of the rain, and put
her lunch on the desk across from Jocelyn. "I got split pea
soup; hope it's still hot."

"No. It's just . . . I was looking over my grandma's papers
and . . . well, this one is a little disturbing."

"Disturbing! That's always good for discussions. Do you
think you'll be able to go through them all today?"

"No, maybe by tomorrow. I'll call you tomorrow, I promise." Shocked by how desperate the page sounded, so different from the ones she'd read earlier, Jocelyn shoved it back
into the bag, doubts about her family's history beginning
to resurface. But her curiosity got the better of her, and
when Laura left the office for a meeting at the main branch
later in the afternoon, she pulled the package out again.

Had she left one man only to be tormented by another—
the "he" mentioned in those first sad pages? Any wonder the
Markham women had such bad luck with men? Leafing
through the stack, she skimmed another.

*His cruelty came in waves meant to beat me down.
Pricks became cuts became wounds too deep for healing.*

*What do you want from me? I have given you
everything I have to give, I would scream at him, and he
would tell me that I knew and indeed I did, but I could
not give him what he claimed he needed to survive.*

*He has asked me for what I cannot give and I cannot
refuse him now, even knowing what I know. Do I have
the will to leave?*

And what could that have been, this thing he would take?
Yet Caprice must have found the will to escape somehow.
Twice. She had escaped twice. It had taken courage to leave
both men, and she had found it. Courage wasn't a quality
Nana France and Constance taught her to associate with
her great-grandmother.

*She had shown up on the porch, a frightened shabby old
woman . . . then disappeared again without saying good-bye.*

Wasn't that what Constance had said? Had she been
frightened of him even after leaving? Had Franklin come
North looking for her? Had she left with him again? Or with
the other one? If that had happened, it would have been an
important part of the narrative that marked Caprice's life;
they wouldn't have left it out. Frantically, Jocelyn shuffled
through the pages, reading a paragraph here, another there,
searching for answers.

Then out of nowhere came Mikela's voice.

"Where were you!" she screamed, dripping wet as she
stamped into the office. "You were supposed to pick me up
from school after lunch. I had a half day today. You were
supposed to pick me up from school! Where were you?"

Snatched into the present, Jocelyn put down the pages and stood up. "Honey, what are you talking about?"

"Don't call me honey! I'm really mad at you, Mom. It was a half day today. You said you would bring me here and I could study here and then we'd go out to dinner. You said that!" A pool of water formed under Mikela's yellow boots, and she stamped her foot, splashing it over the floor.

"Oh, God," Jocelyn muttered. "I must have forgotten. I'm so sorry, I . . ."

"Forgot!" Mikela screamed the word, which echoed through the room and caught the attention of a homeless man sitting at the reading table perusing the local newspaper; he studied them both with an amused, curious grin.

"No! I didn't forget you! Of course, I didn't forget you!" But she had, and Mikela knew it.

"What about last Thursday when you were supposed to take me to the mall?"

"But you were with your father—"

"You said you'd take me to the mall. You forgot that, too, didn't you, that you promised to take me to the mall to get some leggings? You didn't even call."

She vaguely remembered promising Mikela they'd go shopping last Thursday, but the flight was late coming back from Miami, and Asa had insisted that they spent the night at a hotel for the hell of it. "Mikela, I'm—"

"And what about the week before last, and the one before that, and before that?"

"But you said you wanted me to keep you on weekends, not during the week!" Jocelyn offered as an excuse, trying to appease her. "The weekends, Miki, I've been there on . . ."

"You promised those days to me, to make up for the shitty weekends I'm stuck with you. You *promised* me those days!"

"Don't say shitty!"

"I'll say whatever I want to say!"

Stunned by her daughter's rage, Jocelyn stood up and moved toward her, but Mikela drew back.

"Getting ready to hit me again?" she said in a low, taunting voice, just as Mike stepped into the office.

"What's going on?" he said, and Jocelyn dropped her head, embarrassed and ashamed. Mike turned to Mikela. "Go wait for me in the car." Mikela glared at her mother, not moving. "You heard what I said, young lady, wait for me in the car!" Mikela stalked out without a backward glance.

"Did you hit her?" His eyes were wide and disbelieving.

"No, Mike, of course not! You know me better than that."

"I don't know anything anymore. Peaches, what's wrong?" Jocelyn was taken aback by her nickname and the tenderness in his voice

"Nothing." She studied the top hat on the cat in the hat, trying to remember Mikela's laughter when she used to read her the story, and her eyes teared.

"You don't remember to pick our kid up. You give her to me Thanksgiving, Christmas. You don't remember things that are important to her. Don't tell me nothing is wrong!"

She turned to face him. "I'm fine, Mike."

"Everything about you has changed. Your mother's place is a dump. Shit all over the place! Mikela can't stand to go, there's so much crap piled up and laying around. You know what she calls it? The Pig Sty, and that's what it's become. Your mother would turn over in her grave if she saw . . ."

"Mike, you don't know what my mother would do," Jocelyn said, trying to keep control of her voice.

"What's he doing to you, that bastard, whoever he is, who is taking you away from Mikela, from . . ."

"From who? You?" She glared at him incredulously.

"We were over a long time ago, Peaches."

"You don't think I know that!"

"Mikela says you're over there all the time, she says . . ."

"I only see Mikela on weekends," Jocelyn fought back, defensively. "She doesn't know what I do with my time."

"Look at me!" Mike grabbed her shoulders and gently pulled her toward him. Jocelyn glared at him, her eyes hard. "Has this guy got you on something? You look like a fucking junkie! And you know I've seen plenty of them in the business I'm in. Eyes red. Not taking care of your place. Losing weight. You look like shit! He's going to put you out on the street before it's over. Out there like some kind of junkie whore. Who the fuck is he?"

"Oh, go fuck yourself!" Jocelyn snatched away sitting back down. "You don't know what you're talking about. You don't know him. All of you can kiss my ass!"

"Who besides me and Mikela?" Mike asked, his eyes narrowing suspiciously. "Who else is telling you to get yourself together? Who else?"

Laura, entering the small office, slapped her briefcase down on her desk, surprising them both. "You two need to take this mess outside my office!" she said, hands on hips like a disgusted grade-school teacher.

"Oh, God, Laura, I'm so sorry!" Humiliated, Jocelyn avoided Laura's eyes, amazed she hadn't heard her come back in.

"Please go into the conference room. Now!" Heads bowed, Jocelyn and Mike slunk into the empty room.

"Will you give me sole custody?" whispered Mike as Jocelyn closed the door behind them. "I don't want her spending weekends with you, and she doesn't want to anymore. I haven't told you because . . . well, I was hoping things would change. But nothing has."

"What?" Jocelyn said, unbelieving.

"If you can't even remember to pick the kid up, not even in the rain, break promises to her, take her to a filthy house . . . I'm surprised your neighbors haven't called child protective services! If you can't do that, then you need to step the fuck down and give me full custody! I don't want to take you to court to get it, but I will. Don't make me get a lawyer!"

"Full custody?" Jocelyn uttered, even as she heard Asa chanting in her head: Let him have the kid. Let him have the kid.

"You're losing her, Jocelyn. I'm more mother to her than you these days. Don't do this to her."

"No!" Jocelyn said quietly, more to herself than Mike.

Shaking his head in what looked like frustration, Mike opened the door to leave, but then turned to face her, and his tone surprised her. "I'm going to have to do something. If you leave this guy, maybe you'll be okay, and we can talk then, but . . ." He stopped midsentence and sighed, his face softening. "No matter what you say, there's always going to be something between us, you know that as well as I do. Whatever, whoever is messing you up, it's going to be okay." His words were a peace offering, spoken as gently as she'd ever heard him say anything.

Jocelyn nodded reluctantly, recalling the taste of ripe peaches. "Let's try this again," he continued. "Clean up the house so it's fit for a kid to come home to. I'll keep her tonight, but I'll bring her by tomorrow morning around ten. Maybe you can get those leggings she's been wanting. She broke her iPod, so maybe you can pick that up, too, okay? I'll give her some money for it."

"Okay," she said, hardly looking at him, still reeling from what he'd said. "Mike—" She called his name, not sure what she wanted to say, but she spoke too softly; he'd already closed the door.

ASA

First comes the taking of things precious—the blood, the life, the tie to that which holds her. Each day I take more control, and despite your warning, I will take from you what you hold most sacred. There is nothing to keep me from her now. First the blood, the life, the tie.

The three clamor for what she must give willingly, and I cannot appease them for long or they will take her for themselves. Marimba says I owe her, yet hesitates when she speaks. She thinks of you, Caprice, but dares not mention you by name. Her weakness disgusts me.

I despise yet need them, love them as one loves children, and they need me as a child needs a parent, though our love is not familial. Guilt binds me to them for what they gave and what is left of their souls. I've sucked them dry and they demand I give back what I took.

How much do I tell her?

Marimba is the one who truly loved me, yet I am repulsed by what she has become. How she betrayed me—and I have made her pay for that.

How much do I tell her?
Only what she needs to know.

10

his cloven foot

Whatever, whoever is messing you around, it's going to be okay.
Mike's words stayed with Jocelyn as she finished work and
stopped by Whole Foods to buy a rotisserie chicken for dinner. Studying her face in the mirror that night, she realized
Mike was right. Her eyes were sunken and her skin was losing its color. She needed to rest more, get more sun. Take
better care of herself, that was all.

There is nothing messing me around, Mike, she mumbled, as she climbed into bed and turned on the TV to watch
the late news and *The Daily Show*. When it was over, she
flicked on the reading lamp, flipped through old issues of
Essence and *Style*, then turned off the light, gazed at the window, and finally went to see if Asa had come home yet. She
wondered again where he could be, what kept him away so
long. Was he with one of the women he'd been with on
their trips?

Why was she afraid to ask him? What was she scared he
would say? The room was cool, and she checked to make
sure the windows were closed, then got a blanket and threw

it on top of the comforter. She got back into bed and listened, not sure what she was waiting to hear except the noises of the house, ominous as always. The house creaked, and she wondered if someone had broken in. Were footsteps headed to her room? No. It was her mind gone wild. A car alarm went off down the street, and she jumped. She took a breath. It was nothing, just her nerves.

She missed the comfort of knowing Mikela was down the hall, her boisterous cell phone conversations with her friends after she'd gone to bed, the buzz of her computer when she went online. The tension and anger between them had become unbearable. It was a weight that ate away at everything they'd had: their easy affection, camaraderie, a rarity between most mothers and teenage daughters. God knew, she'd never had that kind of relationship with Constance, and she doubted Constance had it with Nana France. But it had come easily to her and Mikela. So much had changed.

Her cell phone rang, startling her, and Luna's name popped on the screen. She nearly answered it, then realized she couldn't take another confrontation. After the fight with Mike, the last thing she wanted to hear was Luna's morbid warnings about her love life. Why couldn't Luna just leave it alone? Was her life so unbearably lonely that she had to insert herself into that of her friends—or friend, since as far as Jocelyn knew, she was the only one. At some point, she'd invite Luna to dinner so she could finally meet this man she talked so bad about. She'd be ashamed of herself then, and rightfully so. And as charmed by him as Jocelyn was.

Whatever, whoever is messing with you.

Unconscious beauty.

For the first time in my life, I'm happy, Jocelyn muttered as she settled under the comforter. She glanced at the clock. Midnight. Asa was never home by midnight.

She closed her eyes, tried for sleep, then remembering the nightmare, prayed it wouldn't come again—that gnawing at her heart like some ravenous rat chewing a path to where it had to go, the dread so deep she couldn't move. Night terrors. Night horrors. Nothing more than that. She made herself think about Asa to chase away the dream, and got hot at the thought of him, then angry at how casually he dismissed her fears. She remembered her daughter's anger, and a heaviness came into her heart.

Maybe Mike was right.

Let him have the kid until we need her again. Asa knew her daughter's name, why couldn't he ever say it? Because of the death of his own. He had been through so much, had given her so much happiness. Why couldn't she just accept him for who he was? She closed her eyes, imagining him running his fingers across her belly, remembering the softness of his tongue. Slipping her hand between her thighs, her fingers deep inside, she caressed herself, imagining the words he spoke when he brought her to climax.

But where did he go?

The thought came suddenly, opening her eyes just as she drifted off into sexual fantasy.

Why wouldn't he tell her?

She sat up straight, sleep gone. Twelve forty-five, and she was wide awake.

There was a bottle of Ambien that had belonged to Constance in the medicine cabinet. She'd gone through a bout of insomnia shortly before she died. Maybe she should take one. That was a quick path to deep sleep. But then she'd be out until eleven the next morning, and Mike was dropping Mikela off at ten, and she didn't want to miss her. After this afternoon, she couldn't be late again. She remembered how Nana France would make warm milk with honey and vanilla for her when she'd been a kid, and it would knock her out before she could finish the cup. A shot of brandy stirred in for good measure would certainly do the trick.

The hall was ice cold and the silence unnerving as she crept downstairs. Had the furnace gone off? It did that sometimes. Upstairs, the attic door slammed shut—and her heart stopped. A random gust of wind from somewhere, that was all. A window not fully closed. Damn this house! Doors slamming for no good reason, lights flickering on and off, it had a mind of its own, always had. If the furnace was out, she sure didn't feel like making her way down those creaky stairs into the dark basement to turn it back on. After Nana France's death, Constance had lived here alone for years. Had Constance ever been lonely, fearful of the silence, disgusted with the creaks and bangs of the house? Had she ever even asked?

Forgive me. Jocelyn felt the weight of guilt fall upon her again. But it was too late for that now—to apologize to her mother, who was gone forever.

She found a clean pot, heated some milk, and poured it into a red mug along with honey, vanilla, and a half cup of brandy, then sat down at the table to savor it. It was hot and burned her tongue; she blew furiously to cool it.

I write for your forgiveness and because I have no choice.

Was she doomed like Caprice to live her regrets?

I will die before I let him have me. I will die before I let him have me. I will not let him have me. For he is a lie and all he has ever been is a lie.

What the hell was Caprice talking about? But a chill shot through her and she trembled. "Damned cold house!" she muttered, knowing it wasn't just the house. But what was it? Dread crept over her. Why had it come?

What had Caprice meant? How do you know a man and not know he is a liar?

When she saw him on Monday, she would ask Asa where he went on weekends, she told herself, promising herself that she would. He demanded enough of her. He had no right to keep it from her. Damn him! She had a right to know. If it was another woman, she wanted to know it.

What about all those fucking whores he spent his time with on the road?

Liar!

The voice came as it had come earlier, not quite in her head but somewhere near where she would be sure to hear it.

Who was the liar? Her or him? Both of them?

Unconscious beauty!

Was she going crazy like Caprice? Like Luna's poor mother? What was her name, Geneva? A string of women with strange names were gathered in her life: Luna, Geneva, Caprice.

Luna and Caprice coming within the same thought sent her back to the brandy for another shot.

She had shown up on the porch, a frightened, shabby old

woman with rotting teeth and a filthy carpetbag stuffed with wrinkled papers and ragged clothes.

But someone had taken the time to read those papers and copy them. Nana France, in a final gesture of love and forgiveness?

On impulse, she grabbed Caprice's pages from her tote bag and headed upstairs, mug of milk in hand. Propping herself on extra pillows, she pulled the comforter to her chin and settled into bed to read.

There were what seemed to be snatches of stories, unconnected and unfinished. It was impossible to see which pages belonged where or how events were related or occurred, where things fell within Caprice's life. A dozen or so pages were filled with lengthy descriptions of homes and people and a few were detailed sketches of elderly white women who must have employed her.

No rhyme or reason, just like her life, Jocelyn thought with sadness.

Stanzas from a poem caught her eye. They weren't in the neat handwriting that distinguished other pages, but printed by hand, as if copied from a book:

> She has taken up her two little babes,
> Kissed them on cheek and chin;
> "Oh, fare ye well, my own two babes,
> For I'll never see you again."

> They had not sailed a league, a league
> A league but barely three,

Until she spied his cloven foot
  And she wept right bitterly.

He stuck the top-mast with his hand
  The foremast with his knee:
And he broke that gallant ship in twain
  And sank her in the sea.

The poem was called "The Demon Lover" and the author was marked unknown. There was an old-fashioned style to it, the rhythm sounded like an Irish brogue when read aloud, so different from Caprice's world, and "leagues" would have been an unknown word to a woman who had never sailed on a ship. Why had she copied this poem and included it?

The page that followed was written by Caprice. Jocelyn read it quickly.

The three seemed dependent upon him for everything—sustenance, money, approval, and he treated them offhandedly like servants or poor relations. Could they be family, I wondered, tied by blood? The two men aped his every gesture, and the woman was servile and devoted but there was a carnal edge to her adoration.

I never knew their names. The youngest was little more than a boy. He was scrawny, with a lean, empty face, and walked with an uneven, hesitant gait, as if crippled. He had a quick smile, when he dared show it, but could never look me in the eye. Of the three, he seemed the most unsoiled. If I tore myself away, I thought I might take him with me, but I suspected it would be too late for that. His face suggested innocence, but there was none to be found. How could there be?

The other was skeletal as well, his face sharp, and his skin had a grayish pallor. His grin was brutish and sly, and the gaze from his slits of eyes frightened me. I dreaded the quick sharp knock on the door that heralded his arrival.

Away from the dim lights of the cabaret, the woman looked younger than she first appeared. There was a reddish, nearly orange cast to her skin and her high, fine cheekbones hinted of Indian heritage, as did the long hair that hung straight down her back. She had enormous but haunted eyes, yet she was the one to whom I felt closest. He had snatched her life from her—or she had given it willingly, God help her wretched soul. At times, she would stand at the door and watch us, silently, her expression empty. A farm girl sees the slaughter of hogs and game, knows the vacant fear in the eyes of animals soon to be butchered. Her eyes were as hollow and dead as any I'd seen. Yet I sensed my plight had touched her.

When would he butcher her, I wondered?

When would he butcher me?

Frantically, Jocelyn searched the remaining pages for another reference to the woman or the other two but found nothing, only half-finished descriptions of places she'd been, writers she'd met, probably before she'd met "him." Perhaps this was nothing more than the beginning of a story, begun and left unfinished. Then she found another passage:

> *He snatched away all things that brought me joy.*
> *The small drawings I sketched of you from memory. My*
> *bits of verse, my books of prose, my journals, and left me*
> *only what he had given me—a diamond pendant,*
> *strings of pearls, that meant nothing. My handkerchiefs*
> *scented with perfume were all I was able to hide.*
>   *He guarded his life scrupulously, even the names*
> *of his tenants were kept secret. A locked door barred*
> *entrance to the upper floors, yet I could hear laughter*
> *and footsteps late at night and early in the morning. My*
> *ears grew keen, like those of a bat, and I knew when he*
> *would join them. He would leave for two days, often*
> *three, then return at dawn, demanding I submit to his*
> *passion. But I had long ago ceased desiring him. He*
> *would try to buy my love with money then, giving me*
> *whatever I asked. Yet when it came to the only thing*
> *I truly needed, the money needed to get you back, my*
> *request was seen as betrayal.*
>   *When I said your name he would slap me, until I saw*
> *the mere mention of you would drive him into a rage.*
> *Could it be the memory of his own children lost so*
> *cruelly? One Sunday morning he smacked my face so*
> *hard that his ring tore my cheek, leaving a scar nearly as*
> *deep as the half-moon upon his own.*

Jocelyn sat straight up in bed. "Goddamn it! Just god-damn it!" she said and ran into the bathroom, opened the medicine cabinet to shake out four Ambien—tiny, blue, harmless-looking—that she downed with the milk left in the mug.

If I can just go to sleep, she said to herself, things will be fine in the morning. If I can just be numb and feel nothing at all.

But she knew the dream would come; that fearful presence would nip at her, make its way up her body until it scratched open her heart. And the words *nearly as deep as the half moon upon his own* whipped her mind until she fell into a deep and terrible sleep.

11

the color gray

It was four in the morning. Luna sat outside Jocelyn's house like a sentinel, smoking Marlboro Lights until they turned her stomach and scorched her throat. She glanced at the moon, as she often did for reassurance. It was a quarter moon tonight, unlike the first time she'd seen him, a sliver of a thing, yet still enough to call him. She dug around the bottom of her purse for loose cigarettes but couldn't find one. Swearing softly, she closed her eyes, opened the window, and drew the cool dawn air deep into her lungs.

The thought had come at midnight. She'd been sitting in her apartment enjoying the silence of night. Pinto, snoring peacefully, had laid his head upon her lap. After an evening of relentless squawking and complaining, Ritz had finally drifted off to wherever canaries went. She'd felt content and happy, ready to fall asleep herself, when suddenly an image of Jocelyn's face, distorted and blurred in gray, entered her mind. She ignored it at first. Pictures coming suddenly from nowhere often meant nothing, and after a moment would simply fade away. She was worried about her friend, and that had probably called it. There were so few people in her small world she tended to be overprotective toward Jocelyn and her family. Perhaps Jocelyn had been troubled or sad earlier in the day or having a nightmare, and somehow she had sensed it. More often than not, when she closed her eyes and shook her head, whatever had come would return to that corner of her mind where such things dwelled.

Not this time. She called Jocelyn then, hanging up quickly when nobody answered. It was Friday night, Mikela was there, and she didn't want to wake them. Most sane people were asleep by now. Only the loonies were up at all hours losing themselves however they could. Loonies, loony tunes. Luna. She chuckled at the thought. That's me, definitely and defiantly loony, she whispered to Pinto, patting his head. She went into the kitchen for chamomile tea to calm her nerves.

But the image came back. As dull and lifeless as newspaper print. Gray, the color of melancholy, of sorrow. Gray, neither black nor white, unsettled, the sucking away of color that meant uncertainty and fear.

It would do no harm, she decided, to drive over there and make sure things were okay, to sit outside the house in her car for a while, see for herself what was going on, and when she was sure that all was fine she would leave with no one the wiser.

So she threw her purple down coat over her pajamas, slipped on her red sneakers, pulled on a black knit cap, and with a quick pat to Pinto's head headed out the door. She parked a block down from Jocelyn's house, lit a cigarette, and prayed nobody would report as suspicious a slightly disheveled black woman in a dirty car parked haphazardly on the curb.

That had been at one, then something wouldn't let her leave so she'd sat, smoking like a crazy woman—waiting for what, she wasn't sure. The good thing was that Jocelyn had returned her call earlier that day, and there was hope in that, particularly after the anger that marked their December conversation. Not even you will ruin this for me, Jocelyn had screamed at her, and Luna knew she could say nothing to convince her. What was there to say?

She shifted her gaze to the house next door, studying the looming structure. It stood back from the road, beckoning her, and she closed her eyes, shutting out its spell. She'd called it right that October night; it truly was a monstrosity. An evil thing. Old houses had spirits, the same as people. And this house spirit was nearly as old as evil itself. At two-thirty, the basement lights had been switched on, then off, and the house went dark; there had been nothing since then. So he must be at home. She glanced again at Jocelyn's house. The second floor lights were off there, too. Jocelyn and Mikela must be asleep. Safe, for the time being.

The boon was wrong again.

"Can't count on the damn thing," she mumbled, rolling up the window. "What good are you if I can't count on you?"

Geneva's voice came to her as clearly as if she were sitting beside her.

Comes when you need it.

"But I need it now, Mama, I need it now."

Use what else you got to make some sense. That's what you do.

And what else did she have? Eyes. Ears, Nose. Fingers. Taste. Thanks to the cigarettes, taste was down for the count. She drummed her fingers on the dashboard in a slow, steady rhythm, thought of listening to the radio, decided against it, and turned on the ignition instead, ready to drive home. Nothing was in Jocelyn's house but those who were there to protect. She was sure of that.

But a minute after turning the key, she turned it off again, held her breath, and listened. Waiting for sound or motion hidden in the quiet. What was she expecting to hear?

And then she heard it. The hum of his car. It came fast, turning corners recklessly. Luna ducked down into her seat, trembling with fear that came abruptly from she wasn't sure where. As he drove closer, she could hear him shifting gears, roughly, with no caution, angrily. He raced down the street, and Luna dove under the dashboard, hitting her head on the steering wheel on the way down. She heard him pull into his driveway and stop. A car door slammed. Was Jocelyn with him? Then where was Mikela? She risked a glance at Jocelyn's window. Maybe she was mistaken, yet she had sensed her friend's presence.

A woman's laugh, coarse and raucous, rang from the end of the driveway followed by harsh words in an ugly, menacing tone. It was his voice, she was sure of that, but the laugh wasn't Jocelyn's and relief swept her. Had he found another victim? But then, as sure as anything, she knew that wasn't true.

She glanced at her watch. Five o'clock. The click of the woman's heels headed down the paved driveway away from the car toward the house. Who was she? Luna wondered, but dared not risk looking; some sense told her to remain unseen, to keep herself hidden from him and whoever was with him.

Someone called to them from an open door. A man's voice, youthful, with an accent she couldn't identify. Cautiously, she peeked over the edge of the dashboard. He drove the car into the garage then walked back outside, closed the door with a remote, and made his way to a side door of the house, taking his slow, graceful time. The woman followed, dipping to one side as if drunk, heels clicking on the asphalt. There was a third one, too, dragging his foot as if crippled. Suddenly, they stopped, as if listening for something, surveying the neighborhood like animals sensing danger. Luna ducked back under the dashboard, uttering a quiet curse, praying she'd parked far enough away from both houses so he wouldn't think her old-ass Mustang had anything to do with him or Jocelyn. She held her breath, as if he could hear it, praying he didn't have that much power. It wasn't until she heard laughter and the tap, tap, tap of the woman's heels down the driveway that she let it go.

Morning came an hour later. There were other noises on the street now—the arrival of the newspaper man and folded papers hitting the sidewalk, early risers on morning jogs, buses pulling away from curbs on nearby and distant streets. The sounds of life and daylight . . . and safety. Only then did Luna turn on the ignition and drive home as fast as she could.

Luna awoke to Pinto licking her face and the ring of her buzzer. Her back hurt, and she had a headache. Her throat was scratchy from all the Marlboros, and her stomach churned. Pushing Pinto aside, she closed her eyes, trying again for sleep, but the buzzer was persistent, and she knew it was no use. Somebody was determined to see her. Stumbling out of bed to answer it, she glanced at the clock. It was noon.

"Luna? You there?" Mike was downstairs. It must be something about Jocelyn.

"Can we come up?" Mikela's voice chimed in with his.

"Sure, give me a minute," Luna said, her voice hoarse from cigarettes. She washed her face, rinsed her mouth with Listerine, and pulled on worn Levi's and an orange t-shirt. A few minutes later, Mike and Mikela sat across from her on her green corduroy couch, Mike nervously sipping a cup of Starbucks coffee, Mikela gobbling blueberry scones Luna had baked the day before.

"Sorry to get you up," Mike said between nervous sips.

"I was just catching a nap." Luna studied his face, noting the worry in his eyes. Mikela, avoiding her gaze, was harder to read.

"Just tell her," Mikela said suddenly, focusing on Luna. "Just tell her, Dad!"

"Guess you wondering why we came over?" Mike asked with a shy, crooked smile.

"The thought crossed my mind," Luna said, smiling reassuringly back at him.

"Just tell her!" said Mikela, voice rising slightly.

"Yeah." Luna glanced at Mikela. "Just tell me."

"I hate her." Mikela bit off half a scone, and Mike threw her a sharp look.

"Don't say that about your mother."

"Well, she hates me!"

"No, she doesn't," Mike and Luna said in unison, and caught each other's eye. In an instant, Luna understood how Jocelyn had fallen in love with him: it was that his eyes were as open as his soul—maybe dangerously so—and let people enter. He had a spacious heart, and that was good—you took in more of life that way, never judging, accepting folks for who they were—but you had to be careful who you let in, Luna knew that much about the seen and unseen.

And for the first time in weeks, she thought about Jerome, long dead, the only man she'd ever loved. That long, serious face and fetching smile, the strength and smell of his body when he lay beside her at night, and above all his laughter when he'd gently tickle as he tried—with no success—to tickle the boon out of her, to lift her from what he called "the moods," those dark places she'd slip to that were impossible to share.

"Jer—" She whispered his nickname aloud without realizing it.

"Excuse me?" Mike said, concerned and puzzled. Luna shook her head, shaking away the thought.

"It's a name I say every now and then. Kind of like a charm."

"Why Jer of all things?" asked Mikela. "That's kind of weird, Luna. Sounds like you're saying jerk. You're acting as weird as she is. What does it mean?"

"It's short for Jerome. He was a friend of mine."

"Was?"

"Don't be fresh!" Mike warned.

"By she, I assume you mean Jocelyn?" Luna said. "That I'm acting weird like your mom."

"Got it!"

"Jerome was my best friend. He meant a lot to me, and every now and then I say his name to make me feel better," Luna said, her voice implying there was no more to be said on the subject.

"Was he your boyfriend?" Mikela persisted.

"Fiancé."

"What happened to him?"

"Died."

"Oh! I'm sorry, Luna," Mikela said, clearly ashamed that she'd pushed her. "He must have been a really nice man if you loved him."

"He was a very nice man."

"Then he didn't drive a silver car." Mikela's eyes narrowed contemptuously with each word.

"You've grown up since October," Luna said in a gentle attempt to change the subject. It had been a long time since that night filled with laughter, pizza, and innocence. Mikela knew something wasn't right, but how much did she know? She'd always been a smart kid, able to read Jocelyn in a wink.

"Silver car?" Mike eyed his daughter curiously, not letting the comment go.

"You've gotten prettier, and taller, and . . . everything, since I saw you last," Luna added, not ready to let Mike in on what both of them knew. Eleven turned into fifteen in the blink of an eye. Boys would come soon, if they weren't already the center of her life, and teenage girls were always nosy and curious about the secret lives of their mothers. Mike shook his head helplessly, and Luna saw that, like most men, he was probably clueless when it came to understanding his teenage daughter.

"So I guess Jocelyn did something that made you angry and hurt your feelings. Want to tell me what it was?"

Mikela shrugged, and Mike answered for her. "Well, she was supposed to be at home this morning—you know, Miki has been staying with her most weekends—and well, we rang her bell at ten this morning, kept ringing it, and she didn't come down, didn't answer it."

"You sure she was there?"

"The car was in the garage. The screen door was locked from the inside, so Miki couldn't use her key. She was there." Mike's face was solemn.

"She didn't want to see me. Same as yesterday." Mikela shrugged nonchalantly, but there was a catch in her voice.

"So what happened yesterday?"

"She was supposed to pick me up at school, in all that stupid rain, and she didn't bother to show up. Forgot about me."

"Forgot?"

Mike nodded his head, disgusted.

"The house is a mess, and it stinks. There's all this crap in the sink. It makes me sick to even be there sometimes. I need to wash my clothes, but there's, like, garbage bags filled with disgusting stuff in the disgusting basement. I hate it there," Mikela continued.

"Things are falling apart?"

"You could say that." Mike nodded.

"Got any more scones?" asked Mikela.

"Why don't you try calling her again? Maybe she over-slept," Luna said to Mike over her shoulder as she headed into the kitchen to warm some.

"I called her before we came over. I was hoping maybe you'd spoken to her, knew what was going on."

Luna didn't want to see the anguish she knew was in his face, so she focused on lining the scones up in a single row in the middle of the cookie sheet, turning on the oven, plac-ing the sheet on the middle rack to warm. She put water in the electric kettle and sorted through her collection of teas for something sweet and calming. She thought again about Jerome, and how nice it would be to have a man in her life, to care for, bake for, make tea for when he was feeling low, and her eyes filled with tears she didn't want anyone to see.

Not for you, my baby. Geneva's voice came from nowhere, even though Geneva had never told her that loving a man was something she could never have. That children would be outside her dream, and the boon was the only gift she would have. Geneva had had more. She'd had a man and a daugh-ter. And look where she'd ended up.

Luna cleared her throat, got rid of the sadness, turned to Mike with a quick reassuring grin. "Don't worry, I'm sure she's fine." She put everything she could into the lie, and Mike nodded, wanting to believe her; she hoped that he did.

When the water was ready, she poured it on a tea ball filled with lemon mist tea in her favorite clay pot, got match-ing cups, and piled the scones on a china plate. Arranging everything on a tray, she headed into the living room. Noticing her struggle with the tray, Mike took it and set it down on the burnished oak chest that served as a coffee table.

"Daddy is such a gentleman," Mikela said, proud but slightly embarrassed.

"Good home training," Luna agreed.

"You can thank my mother, *your* grandma, Miki, for that."

"Other grandma."

"You mad at Miss Constance, too?" Mike asked, amused.

Mikela shook her head with a smile. "Never."

"So will this *gentleman* do me a huge favor?" Luna asked in a saccharine voice. "They had a sale on bottled water at Costco, and I pulled something in my back trying to lug it inside. Would you mind bringing the rest of it in for me?"

Mike hesitated, momentarily puzzled by her request, but when Mikela dropped her eyes to sip her tea, Luna gave a sharp nod in her direction, letting him know she wanted to speak to her alone.

"Sure, let me get it now before I sit down," he said, grabbing a scone and munching it. "Back in a minute."

After he left, Luna watched Mikela dribble too much honey in swirling patterns into her cup. "So what do you know?" she asked.

"Huh?" Mikela glanced up, feigning innocence.

"Don't play with me, Mikela, we're both too grown for that. What's going on with your mom that you don't want to tell your dad?"

Mikela's eyes filled with anger and a sorrow that chilled Luna's heart. "Mom is changing," she said, staring into the cup. "When I'm there, it's like I'm not there, like her mind is somewhere else, and I don't like that guy who lives next door. I don't like Mom . . ."

"Don't like Mom what?"

"Don't like Mom when she's waiting for him. I don't like her when she's with me after leaving him. Something's weird, kind of disgusting about him. She's never forgotten about me before. Never."

Luna leaned forward, directing her gaze into the girl's eyes, into her heart.

"Have you seen him?"

"Who?"

"You know who."

"Yeah, once or twice. I saw him staring at our house when I was coming home from school, like he was thinking about buying it or something. Staring at Mom's room, then at mine. Gave me the creeps. Maybe he's some kind of perv or something."

"Did you tell anybody what you saw?" Mikela shook her head. "Why not?"

"Scared," Mikela said in a voice so low Luna could barely hear her.

"Of what?"

"Him."

"Why?" Luna kept her voice neutral.

Mikela shrugged. "I don't know. I guess I don't like the way he looks at my mom. Like somebody who wants something from her, like he wants to hurt us or kill us or something."

She sees his hunger, Luna thought, the words coming instantly to her. He *was* hungry for something, and that was what the child sensed. Mikela wasn't a teenager yet, there was still enough child in her to see what grown folks didn't want to, to sense a spirit—or lack of one.

"So that was the only time you saw him?"

"No. Daddy and I were in the car and Mom was over his house, and I went into Grandma's house to get something, and I saw him watching me from the window, just watching me, like studying me or something." She paused for a moment, taking a bite from the scone. "He hates me."

"Hates you? Why would he hate you? Don't be silly," Luna said, unnerved by what Mikela had said.

"I don't know why, I just know he does," Mikela replied with certainty, and Luna knew there was no lie she could tell that would reassure her.

"Then make me a promise. Stay away from him. Okay? Promise me that. Stay as far away from him as you can get." *Stay away from him.* The same words Geneva had said to her in nearly the same tone of voice. *Stay away from him.*

Mikela glanced up, fear in her eyes. "Like they used to say to do when I was a kid, that when a stranger wants to talk to you, run away, don't talk back?"

"Yeah, treat him like he's a stranger because that's what he is."

"Is he going to hurt my mom?" Mikela put down the scone, her gaze fastening again on Luna.

Luna buttered a scone, avoiding the girl's eyes. "No, I don't think so. It might not seem like it now, but your mom has good sense. She has kind of a crush on the man, and maybe he does on her. She'll get over it, and everything will be okay."

"What if she doesn't?"

"She will."

"You don't know how it is, Luna. Crush? It's not a crush." Mikela tipped her head and shot Luna a dubious look. "I know what a crush is. I had a crush on Mr. Jones, my science teacher, when I was in fifth grade."

"Despite what is going on, don't forget this: Your mom loves you. She always has and she always will; nothing will come between you. You know that, right?" Mikela didn't answer at once, but after a few moments she nodded, which made Luna smile.

Funny thing about mothers and daughters, how one could sense what was going on with the other no matter what defenses or disguises were put up. Geneva, who was always somewhere in Luna's mind, had tried to hide the power of her boon until it began to destroy them both, and then she had explained all. The mother-daughter bond might be stretched, but it couldn't be broken. How well she knew that.

They ate the scones in silence until Mike rang the buzzer and came back with the bottled water, which the three of them stored in cabinets above the stove and under the sink. Luna threw out the lemon mist and made Mike a pot of Earl Grey, caffeinated as requested, then packed up the leftover scones for them to take home.

"Don't forget that promise," she said to Mikela as she put on her coat. "Remember what I said."

"What promise is that?" asked Mike.

"Between us girls," said Luna.

"I know better than to mess with that." He laughed as they headed out the door. He looked relieved, Luna could see that, and she was happy that he was, although she knew nothing had changed.

Later that night, she wondered if she should warn Mike, call and tell him what Mikela had said, but decided in the end it would do no good. With his vulnerable, open heart, Mike would have no idea what to do. She had to find out more, and time was growing short; Geneva had hinted as much. She was the one who needed to confront this being and take his measure in the only way she knew how.

ASA

How to make you understand? The rarity, complexity, the wonder of it all. The joy of stepping through the portal never to return, to watch it close for eternity. By your own choice. By your own will. By your own hand.

Far better for you to take what is left. Far better to know there will be no one to mourn. Far better to dwell in the world of my making for eternity and have no way back for as long as the Earth will spin.

And you will know that I am as timeless as life. As giving and generous and gracious as anything that can be imagined. With one stroke, gentle or harsh, all will be yours for as long as life goes.

What matters most is for you to give your life so another can live. To make certain that his survival will go on. To make the sacrifice that is called for and needed.

And it is clear that if you will not give, I must take. It will not be the way it was with the others. There is no time now to wait for compliance. There is no time to wait and have done.

My love for you, Caprice, has given way to brutal necessity, and I will not beg your forgiveness.

12

to suck a baby's breath

At ten on Saturday morning, Jocelyn thought she heard a doorbell ring. She tried to wake up, then realized it must be the alarm clock that sat next to her Barbie on the night-stand. Nana France had given her the clock for Christmas so she wouldn't be late for school, as she usually was. The unwelcome buzzing was impossible to sleep through, so she opened her eyes, tried to get up, then remembered she was still sick from that fever she'd had the night before, so she sank back down into her soft, warm bed, swaddled in her pink gingham comforter, and closed her eyes again.

Constance was there, perched on the edge of her bed like she always was when Jocelyn was ill. She could feel her presence and knew she would see her mother if she could just force open her eyes. Constance would be dressed for work in one of her conservative gray lawyer suits, black leather briefcase (the one Jocelyn and Nana France had given her on her last birthday) sitting next to her stylish black pumps, and Jocelyn was so proud of her beautiful, smart mother she opened one eye, just a slit, and heard Constance say, "Hey, Miss Thing, how you feeling this morning? You still feeling sick?" And she nodded and was lost in a dream that made her feel good.

And in a flash, she was at her birthday party, sitting at the head of a long table covered in fancy white lace (Belgian lace, Nana France said). There was laughter all around her, and red, yellow, and pink balloons floating everywhere. The theme music from *Jurassic Park* filled the room, and at the other end of the table was a caramel cake, her favorite and made especially for her, and everyone there was smiling and singing, even her father, who was disarmingly handsome, grinned like Denzel Washington and was dressed in a white linen suit with a yellow rose in his lapel. He hugged her, and she giggled even though she knew he was dead, had died when she was a baby, but he was sitting next to her now and happy and that was all that mattered.

In the distance, she heard Constance say, "I'm on my way to work now, but Nana France is here, so you just call out if you need anything," and somewhere on the other side of the room stood Nana France, red mug in hand, sipping her strong black morning coffee and smoking one of her thin black cigars just lit with her silver lighter covered in roses that Jocelyn loved to touch. "Don't worry about the child, Connie, just a fever," Nana France said, "it will break before noon," and she knew her mother had been there all night, checking her, stroking her forehead, worrying about her, and the love she felt was overpowering as she settled into her dreams, safe and comfortable.

And from the kitchen she smelled the raisin toast Nana France always made for her when she was sick. It was always heavily buttered and lightly burnt, so she had to watch out for the raisins that were hot and burned her tongue, and along with the smell of raisins came the scent of Chanel, lingering as it always did whenever they were around.

"Mom?" Jocelyn said, floating high above the bed, her little-girl voice coming from deep within her, "Mommy, you still here?"

"Always," Constance said, and Jocelyn tried to stay awake as she waited for the buttered toast and milky tea Nana France would soon bring on a wooden tray. And she floated back to sleep.

At two in the morning, Jocelyn sat up in bed, glanced at the clock, and realized she'd slept through one full day and into the next, missing Mike and Mikela. He'd brought her at ten and she'd slept right through it. She tried to stand up, holding on to the edge of the bed, then fell down overcome with dizziness.

"I'm sorry, Miki," she wailed, standing up long enough to make her way into the bathroom. Bending over the toilet, she jammed her finger deep into her throat, senselessly trying to throw up any of the pills that were left, but gagged and collapsed on the bathroom floor. She lay there for a minute counting tiles on the floor, then dragged herself back to bed. Pages from Caprice's manuscript were spread on the comforter. Unwilling to look at, or even think about them, she pushed them onto the floor, trying to forget what she'd read the night before.

She pulled the sheets and covers over her head, closed her eyes, and desperately tried to return to the dream and her mother sitting patiently on the edge of the bed, and for a moment she caught a whiff of Nana France's cigar and could taste in the back of her throat the raisin toast and weak milky tea spiced with honey and cinnamon. Sleep finally came, fitful and disjointed, and she awoke an hour later, temples throbbing, legs jerking as if she had run ten miles. It was still dark outside, so she knew it must still be Sunday, and she thought about Asa because that was when he came home.

Pulling herself out of bed, she went to the window to see if his car was there. When it wasn't, she reminded herself that he always parked in the garage. Could he be home? Would she feel his presence? He always said she had a sense about him, that they were two of a kind, who belonged together always, and no matter where she was he would find her no matter where she hid, like the little rabbit in *The Runaway Bunny* story she used to read Mikela, and that thought made her smile uneasily. She stumbled back to bed, trying to escape again into the dream, but it was gone. There was only the tightening in her stomach and the dizziness that kept her from thinking straight.

Coffee would help. She would make strong black coffee like Nana France drank to wake her up, chase away the grogginess. And a shower. She would take a shower, then go downstairs and make some coffee. And when sober and straight, she would call Mike and Mikela. What would she tell them? Her mind raced with lies. That she was sick. Yes, in a way she was. All that rain and Mikela's anger and Mike's disgusting accusations had beaten the life out of her. She *had* felt sick. So she'd taken some medicine that had made her sleep. Made her sleep longer than she meant to because she had taken too much. Accidently taken too much. That was why she hadn't awakened. But maybe Mike hadn't brought Mikela by. Maybe she hadn't missed them. There was no need to make excuses if they hadn't come, if she hadn't missed them. He had said ten, but had he rung the bell? It had seemed so real, the alarm clock parked like it always was near her old doll. God, what was wrong with her?

So she would talk to Mikela and promise to make it up. She would clean up the house and they would go shopping. To the mall for clothes. No, she wanted red leggings; no, black ones, and new sneakers. Nikes, she'd said. Or had she given her that for Christmas? Or maybe they'd go to Best Buy for a new iPod—Mike said that was what she needed, or was it something else electronic? An iPad, maybe? But she couldn't afford an iPad; didn't Mike say he'd give her the money for an iPad? She'd pick her up after school today. Except it must be Sunday and there was no school. No, she'd sleep until two, get up, and pick her up at three. Tomorrow afternoon. Monday afternoon.

No! Monday was her day back with him, and she wasn't working this week. It was the day she went to him, and they would go off somewhere, maybe Atlantic City again, that was close enough to drive—or fly, somewhere distant, like he said they'd go if she didn't come back to work. How could she go on Monday? How could she leave him, then? It would need to be another day. That was all. But when? No day this week. They might go to Negril again. No, no, that man again, please not that man with his putrid smell and callused hands. No, he'd promised her San Francisco. He'd promised that.

She pulled herself up to take a shower, nearly tripping on the bathroom rug bunched around the toilet. Turning the shower on full force, she got in and soaped herself with the pink Dove soap she'd bought for Mikela, but the showers she took with him came back as she touched those parts he caressed with his lips and tongue, and she caught her breath as she imagined his fingers inside her, taking from her what she sometimes didn't want to give again but always did, him pulling it from her in any way that he could.

She had to see him.

One Sunday morning he smacked my face so hard that his ring tore my cheek, leaving a scar nearly as deep as the half moon upon his own.

No! It couldn't be the same. What craziness was that? Ridiculous coincidence. How stupid to be scared of that. Like some dumb kid.

Disoriented, she wrapped herself in a towel, went back to bed, picked up the phone to call Mike, then put it down before it rang. What time was it, past two now? This was crazy. They'd be asleep. She didn't feel like hearing that drug mess again. A fucking junkie! How dare Mike call her that. Mike would think the worst of her if she called him now. She didn't want to hear the disappointment in Mikela's voice. But she'd be asleep anyway. She thought about Asa. What was he doing? What time did he get home? He was always there on Monday mornings when she went to him. She looked out the window again. A light was on in the house. The kitchen light. So he was home now, back from wherever he had been.

You're pitiful. Absolutely pitiful.

It was Nana France, accusing and disappointed, shaking her head as she smoked her thin cigar.

But I'm in love, Nana France.

You're in crazy!

"Leave me alone, both of you," Jocelyn said, to voices that weren't there. The fear he would leave again before she could see him overwhelmed her. Forget about the coffee; she needed to see him now. This minute. No time to wait. She pulled on jeans, sweater, a coat, and headed out the back door.

Her hair was still dripping wet from the shower, and a chill seeped through her body, making her shiver as she made her way down her driveway to his back door. She'd surprise him. She saw with relief the kitchen light was still on, so he hadn't gone to bed yet. So this was when he came home, before dawn while she was asleep. It was good to know that. She would remember it, something else about him she had discovered. He kept secrets. Damn him and all his secrets! And this was one of them. What were the others?

She had a key to the back door but not the front. They had exchanged keys three weeks after they'd slept together—they both lived alone, so it was good to know someone could get in if it was necessary, they decided. It bonded them in a way she liked, that easy access to each other; he would never bring a woman home if he knew she had a key. She'd never had to use it. The screen to the back door was always open on Monday mornings when she came. He was always waiting for her.

It was locked tonight. Why not? He had no idea she was coming. She'd have to go to the front and ring the bell. He'd promised a front door key weeks ago, so she'd always feel she belonged there, that was what he'd said anyway, but he never gave it to her, and she forgot to ask.

A light was on upstairs. Strange. She'd never known him to work at night—work at all. *Don't trust a man who won't tell you how he makes his money!* She paused before ringing the bell; something held her back. Should she go back home, stick to the ritual they'd set up, their Monday through Friday ritual? Why break it now? It *was* Monday morning, after all, but if she went back home she could go back to sleep and return refreshed and ready for him later in the day, happy to go anywhere he wanted to take her. On an adventure. Like always.

She turned to leave but paused. Was someone moving around inside? She moved closer to the door, then stopped. The door was thick, but she could hear noises coming from a window left open in the kitchen. Was it laughter, a woman's laughter? But it could simply be the laugh track from some silly TV comedy, although she'd never known him to watch TV; he was dismissive of it. And laugh tracks were never just one person, and canned laughter never had this touch of hysteria, this shrillness.

"Asa?" She called his name, as if he might hear her through the door. Nothing stirred. Quiet again. She knocked hesitantly, felt as if she were begging entrance, and when there was no answer, she screamed his name, rang the bell repeatedly. "Asa! Asa!"

He opened the door, reluctantly it seemed.

The stench stopped her short. It was not the sweet, subtle smell of amber or jasmine she had grown used to but the pungent stink of death—of animals left to fester on the road, human flesh turned gray in decomposition. It was a smell one never forgets, Nana France always said, life gone to decay. It dug its way inside her, made her retch, cover her mouth and nose, draw back into the freshness of the early morning. He stared at her, his dark eyes bright with rage.

"I—I—saw a light," she stammered, determined not to apologize, but apology was in her voice, which came out thin and ashamed. She had never felt diminished by him before, not even with the men in the islands or the things he had done to her in bed, but she was humiliated now, and that feeling blocked everything else—even the smell seemed less. She felt dizzy again, falling into the dream again. She must still be lying in her bed, had never left the house. She could even make out Nana France standing behind him, eyes focused on her curiously, dragging on her thin cigar.

"Nana France?" she said, blinking to focus, her vision blurred and hazy.

But it wasn't Nana France who stepped from the shadows into the dimly lit room. It was a woman with skin the color of apricots and black hair hanging long and limp straight down her back, a skinny woman blowing smoke in short quick puffs. Her haunted eyes fastened on Jocelyn, and Jocelyn knew that even if she wanted to scream, she couldn't, that the woman would steal her breath. Wasn't that what Nana

France said about cats, that they could suck a baby's breath, nuzzle close, lap milk left on her chin, crouch low upon her chest, then pounce, mouth greedily holding the baby's lips until she died. Would she suck *her* breath like a cat? Hold it until *she* died?

"You're here now. Come in," Asa said stiffly, as if inviting an intruder into an intimate, private party. Afraid of the woman, Jocelyn stood still, not moving. "Come." His voice became gentle, welcoming, as it always was. He held out his hand, and she moved toward him, hesitantly stepping into the tight, fetid corridor as if still in a dream. The woman giggled lightly, like a child who has stolen something for which she will be punished, but then her eyes darkened, filling with sadness. She reached out toward Jocelyn with clawing fingers and sharp nails as bloody red as those roses he had sent her, but Asa grabbed her hand, pulled it away from Jocelyn, crushing her fingers until Jocelyn heard the dull snapping of her bones as he stared ahead with a cruelty in his eyes she had never seen. Others came then, circling the woman like hungry children—a boy who limped, a man with a clownish, wolfish grin.

Could they be family, I wondered, tied by blood? The two men aped his every gesture, and the woman was devoted, but there was a carnal edge to her adoration.

Caprice's words came to Jocelyn then, along with an answer—his answer.

In a manner of speaking, we are, he said, *or* Jocelyn thought she heard him say. *Or* did he speak at all, had she imagined it? How could he read her thoughts? His lips hadn't moved. The voice that spoke wasn't his, or was it? Where were the words coming from? Somewhere inside where they hadn't been before. She must still be in the dream, asleep in her bed, imagining it all.

"I don't feel well. I took too much medicine to make me sleep, and it made me sick," she muttered, and he pulled her to him, burying her face in his chest.

"Nothing exists for you but me. Nothing is here but me," he whispered in her ear. "I'm taking you up upstairs now, and when you wake in the morning we'll talk and then you'll understand."

"Understand?" she said, head still buried in a chest that caved into itself, yet she could hear no heart.

She closed out everything that made no sense as he walked her upstairs, stair by stair as if she were a wounded child. He laid her out on his bed, undressed her, climbed in bed beside her, touching her all over, and as she fell asleep she remembered his words and wondered what they meant.

13

a soul, as well

When Jocelyn awoke the next morning, she knew the night before must have been a dream. The offensive stench was gone and the room was cool and fresh, as familiar as it had always been, smelling sweetly of amber and jasmine. The pale blue sheets were cool and smooth against her skin, and golden sun poured in through the window, bright and warm. Asa sat beside her on the bed, much as her mother had in her dream, and she felt as if she were back in that protected place. He kissed her lightly on the forehead, and she sighed, relieved and happy, grateful that a new day had begun.

They sat comfortably in each other's presence, she in his black silk pajama top, he in the bottoms—like happy newlyweds in a hotel commercial, she thought, and smiled to herself. He must have slipped it on her while she was asleep. His voice was soothing and calm when he spoke, like a parent telling a child a bedtime story; she closed her eyes, listening as a child does, trusting and sleepily attentive.

She'd heard the voice before, usually the morning after some wild escapade or another, on which she'd followed him, no questions asked. Or upon returning to their room after a night with one of the nameless painted girls, who spoke little and gazed at her blankly, after they'd satisfied him in some way he never explained. It was a sweetly apologetic voice, one that told her she was about to hear something she couldn't believe.

"I need to tell you something, and I don't want you to be afraid of me; more than anything else, I don't want to lose you."

"Why would you lose me?" She yawned, slightly bored, but snuggled closer to him. "Game time?" she asked, because he loved playing games.

He chuckled then, good-naturedly, as reassuring as it always was when he became melancholy. "I love you Jocelyn, but I often wonder how deeply you love me. Really love me." He'd never said that before, and his words puzzled her. Sitting up, she searched his face for an answer.

"How, after all this time, could you ask me something like that?" She didn't say, after all the things I've done with you.

"I need to know." His voice was abruptly demanding, cold. She'd heard that one, too, although not as often as the other because she rarely refused him, and it came only when he wanted something she didn't want to give.

She turned away from him, focusing instead on the black-and-white photograph of the Giza pyramids that hung on the opposite wall. He'd been to Egypt, one of the many places he said he wanted to take her and a place she'd always dreamed of going. She was a lost for a moment in the fantasy of it, how it would be to stand and see something so remarkable, something she'd only seen in photographs. Giza, the Great Wall of China, the Taj Mahal—the wonders of the world he'd promised her someday.

"Listen to me!" He grabbed her chin, forcing her to look into his eyes.

"Why are you doing this?" she said, stunned and angry.

"I don't have a choice."

"What do you mean, you don't have a choice?"

"It's come to this," he said. "There's no more time."

"Time for what?"

"What has to be."

She glanced at the window, gazed at the sun, imagining the warmth that came with it. She remembered the dream that must not have been a dream, and fear shot through her. "Does this have something to do with last night?" she asked, afraid.

He closed the blinds, and the room was shadowed in darkness.

"It's about that, isn't it. It wasn't a dream. Where are the others? Who were they?"

"What others?" He sat back beside her, no answer in his eyes.

"The ones who were here when I came last night."

He shook his head impatiently, a parent scolding a dis-obedient child. "I told you then, all that was in your mind. Your imagination. I told you that before."

The three seemed dependent upon him for everything— sustenance, money, approval, and he treated them offhandedly like servants or poor relations.

Had Caprice's words buried themselves so deeply inside

her mind that she gave them credence, turned them into reality? Had everything that happened last night, all she had seen, been only in her mind? She felt panic, then fright.

When he got in these moods, unpredictable and spiteful, she wanted to be away from him, leave and go back home for a while, despite the mess, and she felt that way now. She snatched her jeans off the floor and pulled them on, but he grabbed her hand, gently but unyielding. She knocked it away, but the look in his eyes made her stop. Was she scared or simply angry? They seemed the same; there was no way to read him this morning.

"I'm going home," she said.

"Can't let you go. Not again. It's beyond that now."

"Beyond what, Asa? I don't understand what you're talking about. Talk sense!" She yanked her jeans up over her hips and fastened them, pulled on her sweater, smoothed her hair down with her hand. It was damp still and fell down her back in spiraled curls. He touched, then pulled one.

"Have I ever told you how much I love your hair?"

"Beyond what?"

"Sit down. Just what I said, Jocelyn. I will not let you leave me." She sat back down, facing him, her eyes searching his. "Because . . ." He paused. "Because I need to tell you more about me. You need to know who I am . . . what I am."

"*What* you are?" Half-amused, she narrowed her eyes and grinned. "What are you talking about?" She searched for, and expected to see, a glint of laughter in his eyes. They played like that sometimes, pretending. His games always had hints of danger and jeopardy, like the time he tried to convince her he had murdered a woman in New Orleans, and was capable of anything, so she'd better be careful. He described what he'd done in detail, how he'd strangled her, and how her eyes had popped and her breath had gone, and he'd frightened Jocelyn to the point that she almost believed him, because there was nothing in his eyes, and he'd begun to weep as he put a silken rope around her neck and began to pull it. And then he had thrown back his head in gales of laughter, tossing the rope on the floor, teasing her about believing every word.

"I guess there's a sucker born every minute," she muttered, and then joined him in his laughter.

And the time he'd convinced her he was wanted by Interpol for passing bad checks. He'd even pulled up a Web site showing his name, but that was another game, and he'd given her a pearl necklace to commemorate that one, claiming he'd stolen it from Tiffany's. He was a great one for games, teasing her, making fun of reality, so she poked him playfully in the ribs. "What you are? Are you trying to scare me or something?" But a shiver crept up her back.

"The truth about me, that's all. I'm not what I seem."

What of you is true?

Caprice's words again, in a voice that sounded vaguely like Nana France's, rang inside her, and he lifted his head as if he heard it, his eyes growing fearful. When was the last time she had seen him afraid? The first time he entered her house, when he glanced toward the stairs? That memory suddenly came back to her.

"My great-grandmother Caprice knew a guy like you." She threw it out with a slip of a smile, settling back down on the bed, joking and joining him in his game, whatever it was, but she noticed he had flinched at the mention of Caprice's name. "And he was bad, *bad* news. I hope I haven't run into his great-grandson or something! Wouldn't that be all I need, to run into some distant relative!" she grumbled, half in jest as she knelt on the floor, looking for her shoes, pulling on her socks instead. They belonged to Mikela, reminding her that she still had to answer to her daughter. She felt stronger now; the sleep had done her good, and she was ready to face what she had to. "Listen, I'll see you later, Asa. I got to get home and get some rest. Clear my mind. Those pills I took really messed me up."

"And what if I told you I was that man," he said. "The man your great-grandmother loved."

"Come on," she said, not hiding her annoyance that he wasn't taking her seriously. "Do you expect me to believe something like that? Stop playing with me! I'm tired. I want to go home."

"What if I swore on everything I hold sacred, my love for you, my love for her."

She smiled, patronizing him. "I'd think you got hold of some bad dope. Stay away from that meth, baby, it's fucking up your mind."

"This isn't funny! Don't you believe there is more to life than you can know or see? That there are things that go beyond your understanding and your knowledge? Think about that, Jocelyn, and tell me the truth." He spoke slowly, rationally, and she stopped what she was doing, unsure of what to do but willing to listen.

There were things in her life, after all, that were not easily explained—meeting him, for one thing, in the way she had, when she desperately needed something to give her life meaning; Nana France's voice floating in when she least expected to hear it. Luna, who admitted that her life was made up of mysteries and enigmas, could attest to what he said. She'd be right at home in this conversation. Jocelyn almost chuckled when she thought about what Luna would make of this.

"I wouldn't believe you," she said, but what she meant was, I don't want to believe you, I can't allow myself to believe you. Yet a corner of her heart wanted to keep playing, to understand what he was trying to say, where he was going with this. His eyes drew her in as they always did, and she remembered the eyes of those troubled kids she'd once worked with, the children only she would listen to and understand. So she settled down beside him, again aware of how comfortable she still felt with him. How easy it was to hear everything he said, to believe it. He was that convincing. He was, after all, the man she'd loved for so many months, she reminded herself, who had led her places, dark and frightening at first, where no one had ever taken her and where she would never go on her own, and he'd always brought her back unscathed, wiser for the going. At least in some ways. So much had been surrendered to him. How could she not listen?

"If you want me to, I can tell you things about Caprice. Shall I tell you?" He was begging, and that was unsettling. He'd never begged before. This was a new one, and she didn't like to see him this weak, begging like this. She stared straight ahead as he continued. "She came to New York running from a man who beat her cruelly. She lived above a butcher store before she lived with me. She . . ."

"Stop it!" He was treading on ground that didn't belong to him. Using her family against her for his games. She searched his eyes for any truth she could find but saw nothing.

"There are things about me that even I don't understand. Why this happened to me when it did—so long ago—why I am the way I am, why what I need to . . . to continue living is what it is. I just know it is necessary. I've always known. And it is only through your love, unyielding and unconditional, that I can continue as I do."

Jocelyn studied his face, the way he held his body, unsure whether to be afraid or simply laugh at him for putting her on. Yet there was the scar, that half-moon on his face, and she examined it now—how deeply it cut, how long it must have been there. That was true. Or was it? She had read it in Caprice's words. Were they meant for her to discover, like Luna said? Were they a warning? Or had Caprice's papers been published somewhere else, years ago, unknown to her family? Or had he scarred his face to blend into some story line before he met her? But that was ridiculous. It made no sense at all.

"I do know one thing," he continued, his eyes not leaving hers. "I know that I love you, and you will always be with me. You and she are the same to me. You have given me the chance she took away, and I can't let it happen again."

"I am not Caprice," she said, doubtful and fearful, and wondering for the first time if he could be crazy. He had called her Caprice once or twice when they made love. She'd asked him about it later, and he had denied it, saying she was her own woman and he loved her for who she was, yet there was something in the way he said it, something in his eyes. Was he insane? But she would have known it by now, wouldn't she? Something would have given him away.

"Take pity on me, Jocelyn, can't you see who I am, what I am?"

He buried his face in his hands, turning away from her. She had never seen him so vulnerable, and his helplessness disarmed her. Crazy or not, she realized she loved him, wanted to comfort him. She pulled his hands away from his face, then took his chin and made him look into her eyes, just as he'd done to her earlier.

"Then tell me who you *really* are," she said neutrally, suspending belief, humoring him and wondering what he would say.

"Whoever I need to be, whoever you need me to be."

"That's no answer!"

"I will tell you things about me that I have told no living being. I am not like most people. I don't measure my life in years or months or days or hours, but in decades, in a century." He pulled away, still holding her hand, caressing it. "I am infinite, in a way. With no beginning or end, no periods or commas. Nothing to keep me here or there. Do you understand what I am saying?"

"What of you is true?" She asked Caprice's question without realizing she'd said it.

"I have been truthful with you. I told you that first day that I was older than I looked," he said with a touch of humor, and Jocelyn, despite herself, gave a slight, hesitant smile. "I have never lied to you. Except for one thing. Only one, when there was no choice, but not anymore. From this day forward, I'll keep nothing from you."

"What one thing?"

"Marimba's children were not mine. They belonged to her."

"Why did you lie about that?"

"To convince you to stay."

"Because you knew your story would touch me?"

He nodded. "How else could I get you to love me?"

"But there was a Marimba?"

"She loved me with all of her heart. Please forgive me for my lie."

When he took her hand, she remembered the first time he touched her, and reminded herself that he was the man she had known for the last six months, made love to, sharing everything about herself she could. Or was he? She had listened, yet couldn't make sense of what he was saying. Was he crazy? Was she?

"Souls go forward in different forms, at different times, and you are Caprice. I knew it the moment I saw you." He kissed her lips lightly, as if asking a question, and she responded because she always did, because it was her habit. His touch was the same; the lips, the thrill that she felt were the same.

"Are you happy with me? Tell me?"

She remembered how lonely she had been before she met him. How empty she had felt, how unloved and unhappy. Her life had changed because of him, and he had become the most important thing in it. Wasn't this what love was supposed to be?

"Yes," she said after a moment's hesitation.

"Can you really live without me? I am doomed without you."

"I don't know," she said, but that corner of her heart that he had entered bid her to say yes.

"I can see into your soul, Jocelyn. You are as tied to me as I am you. There is nowhere that you can go that I will not be with you."

"I've told you so many times that I love you. Isn't that enough?"

He shook his head. "You must prove it." An oddly menacing tone had crept into his voice that alarmed her.

"Prove it? How do you need me to prove it?" She didn't hide the doubt in her voice.

"How deeply do you love me, Jocelyn? With all your heart? Then you must give me your soul, as well."

"My soul?"

"To be with me forever, until the end of time. One quick stroke, and it will be done for all eternity. One stroke, or two, perhaps, to cut what holds you here."

"And what holds me here?" she said, but knew that he was talking about her daughter, about Mikela.

Filled with disgust turned to dread, she drew away from him, gazing at the window, trying to see the sun through the darkened shades, but could see no clouds or sky; the sun had gone. He touched her arm as if trying to get her attention. She tried to pull away but somehow couldn't.

What was a soul anyway? The question came to her

abruptly. Why not just tell him what he wanted to hear? She didn't have to mean it. Yes, you can have that, too, as I have given you my body and my heart? They were just words. What was a soul but something they talked about in church? Was she even sure she had one? Why not simply say it, and settle down beside him, feel his body strong inside hers, as she always had, and love him with no boundaries? Stay with him until eternity. Play this game, too. Except for that one thing he had just said. She glanced at him doubtfully.

"There can be nothing left of you but me," he said. "That is my condition."

"What do you mean? 'Nothing left of you but me'?"

"Just what I said, listen to me. Listen to me, Jocelyn."

"No! Tell me what you mean, exactly what you mean. No bullshit, Asa, just say it!"

Annoyance flickered in his eyes. "Is it that hard to understand, that I need every part of you, completely. Not just a bit, the whole thing. That's what I love, that's what I need. You can't leave *anything* behind."

No, he couldn't mean that. She felt a tickle at the base of her skull.

"Do you mean like property or . . . ?"

"No, Jocelyn, I don't mean like fucking property. I mean *you*. What's attached to *you*. What *you* gave life to."

"Like what Marimba did with her children?"

The tickle left her skull and skittered down her spine.

"You expect me to kill myself and my daughter to join you in your craziness?" she screamed incredulously. "Are you out of your fucking mind?"

He smiled saying nothing.

"I need to go home. I don't believe you." She'd meant that she didn't believe where he had gone with this; there was no way she could believe what he'd had just told her. This was beyond sanity and belief.

"I know," he said, "but you will." He pulled her to him, holding her against him, and she felt the familiar sexual tug, but for the first time she felt something else as well: terror. "You know the truth of me. What I am and what I need from you."

What of you is true?

He pulled her body into his, gently kissing her throat and breast in the way he knew she loved.

"No!"

"For now," he said.

❧

"What do you want from me, I have given you everything I have to give," I would scream at him, and he would tell me that I knew, and indeed I did, but I could not give him what he wanted to survive.

Caprice's words wouldn't leave. They clung to her as she ran from his house into her own, when she closed her back door—locking the screen and the door behind her. She found the red flannel robe her mother had bought her some years ago from L. L. Bean and wrapped herself inside it, but the thickness didn't lessen her trembling.

She thought about Mikela and realized there was still

time for Mike to bring Mikela for the visit she'd lost. She needed to warn him. So that was what Asa had meant before about "letting him have the kid until we needed her."

"Mike!" she screamed into the phone when he answered. "Mike!"

"Peaches, you okay? Where the hell have you been? We came by yesterday morning, and you didn't come to the door. What's going on? Tell me."

"Mike, I'm . . ." She paused, unable to say what she was feeling or be honest about what was happening in her life. Mike couldn't understand, she was sure of that. How could he possibly understand when she didn't? How could he accept what she'd gotten herself into? "I've just had a kind of a rough weekend, I . . . couldn't sleep, so I took some of my mother's old sleeping pills."

"What did you take?"

"Ambien? I just took a couple . . . I . . ."

"A couple!"

"Anyway, they kind of knocked me out. I'm fine now."

"How many did you take?"

"I . . . don't want to go into it."

"Oh, Christ, Peaches! Have you lost your mind? But you're okay now, right?"

"Yeah. I am now."

He paused. "No, you're not. You can't lie to me." But she had lied to him, so many times about so many things, and he had believed her.

"I'm okay now. Is Mikela okay?"

Another pause.

"She's fine. She's in school. Do you know what time it is?"

"I . . ."

"It's three. Why don't we wait until next week, and I'll bring her by then. This weekend was rough on her, too."

"I'm sorry, Mike." She cried softly, holding the phone far away from her mouth so he wouldn't hear her. "I'm so sorry."

"Who is hurting you, Peaches? Tell me and I'll . . . I'll do whatever I need to do to take care of you, make it okay."

She smiled despite herself, recalling her mother's assessment of Mike's ability to take care of anything, even himself. "I just need to make sure Mikela is okay, that she is safe."

"She's fine. Next Friday, I'll bring her by, like always. Do you want her to stay with you for a while? Like maybe for a week or so? You need to spend . . . more time with her."

"No!"

"Let him have the kid until we need her again. Leave her until then. What else do you need?"

"Tell her I love her, okay? . . . Will you do that for me, please, tell her that?"

"You know I'm here if you need anything, you know that, don't you?"

"I know," she said, hanging up before he could ask anything else.

14

as beast needs flesh

Mike called just before Luna dozed off. The Science Channel had drowned out the moans of the couple next door, whose noisy lovemaking had been amusing then annoying, and a talking-heads discussion about Jupiter's moons was lulling her to sleep. Her memories of what she'd seen at the man's house the week before still frightened her, and she tried not to think about it. She was good at putting things out of her mind when she needed to, and God knew she needed to forget that. Besides, Mike had left a message on Monday morning saying he'd heard from Jocelyn, and she was fine. It was best, Luna decided, to wait for Jocelyn to reach out to her, simply let things be. Maybe it wasn't as bad as she'd thought. It had been four o'clock in the morning and maybe her mind had played tricks.

And then came Mike's call.

"Hey, Luna? It's me . . . uh, well, I wanted to get back to you about something that's been bothering me since I left the message, and I . . ."

"It's Jocelyn!" she interrupted him, alarmed by his stammering. "What's going on?"

"Well, I think this guy she's involved with . . . you know, the guy who lives next door? I don't know if she's mentioned him to you, but—"

"I know who he is."

"I'm her ex, and you probably think this is none of my damn business, but I can tell when something's not right, and she was crying on the phone, Luna. Crying! She tried to hide it, but I knew she was."

"Tell me what she said." Luna was impatient.

"Didn't sound like herself. Said she just wanted me to tell Miki she loved her, to keep her safe. I'm worried about her. So, do you know anything about this dude she's been seeing, the one who lives next door?"

"No," Luna answered quickly.

"Then I'm thinking maybe I should hire a PI, get somebody to find out something about him. I don't even know what his last name is. If he even has a last name. Maybe he has just has one name, like a thug. Think he could be a drug dealer or something, living in that big house all by himself? Every time I see her, she looks like she's high on something."

"I doubt that, Mike. That he's a drug dealer."

"Where does he get all that money then? Do you know about any legitimate business he owns?"

Luna understood enough about the hiding, saving, and spending of large sums of money to know how easily one could gain wealth over decades and move it through countless accounts in dozens of nations without putting in a personal appearance. Global financial laws were notoriously lax. There was no limit to how easily a wealthy man could transport and conceal his money.

"Not every rich man with no ties is a drug dealer, Mike."

"I know that but, well, the way he's showed up all of a sudden and . . . well, do you think a PI is a good idea?"

There wasn't a PI in the world who could find out anything worth knowing about this man. "No, Mike, I don't. Why don't you let me see what I can find out from Jocelyn? She and I have been friends a long time. She'll tell me things she might not tell you."

"Luna, I don't know, I . . ."

"Please, Mike. Let me talk to her first. Just take care of Miki, and maybe you should . . . keep an eye on her closely, keep her close to home, that kind—"

"You think Miki is in some kind of danger?"

"No." She quelled the panic in his voice. "But you know how teenage girls can be."

"I'll call you if I hear from her again, okay?"

"Yeah, no matter what time it is." After he hung up, she lay in bed thinking about what Mike had said, knowing it had finally come down to doing what she'd been fearing.

It would do no good to go tomorrow. It had to be now. Tonight. He would have slipped into his mask by morning, burying that part of him that only she could see. Night was when he would come into his own, a time to prey upon the vulnerable, bask in the presence of those who surrounded him—the ones she had seen him with last Saturday. It was midnight. She'd wait a few hours, until the world was quiet, and then she'd leave. In order to find out what she had to know, she needed to view him at his strongest.

Geneva's ritual herbs and gems were kept in a blue silk sack hidden in a cedar box underneath her bed. She felt a sense of dread as she crawled under the bed to retrieve them, wishing she could go back to bed, become a normal woman with a sleepy dog and noisy parakeet that kept her awake, even though she knew there was no chance of that.

Old memories came back as she opened the drawstring: Geneva's anger when she packed the herbs, anger that always seemed to come from nowhere—had her mother felt about the boon and all the gifts it brought as strongly as she did? The bag was made of fine Thai silk, the most expensive her mother could afford, and she remembered her reverence as she blessed or touched each charm and the ecstasy in Geneva's eyes when she tied a pendant, always unwanted, around her daughter's neck.

Geneva replaced the herbs monthly, but Luna never did, despite her mother's urging—did you get them herbs, my baby, did you get them herbs—whispered nearly every time she saw her. Luna bought or found new ones only when she thought they might be needed, which was seldom. Yet some sixth sense (the boon, again) had forced her to make those pilgrimages to Brooklyn and Chinatown at the beginning of the year to replenish what was needed.

The frail Asian woman in Chinatown had painstakingly measured and sniffed each requested herb before carefully placing them in a paper bag and giving Jocelyn a knowing wink. Brother Cedric in Brooklyn, an elderly Rasta with gray dreadlocks that flowed gracefully to his shoulder, said nothing as he filled her requests but slipped a card into her bag with the names of those who might "offer aid" if she needed it. She thanked him, and they'd chatted amiably about the phases of the moon before she left. She smiled now as she thought of the two of them. Maybe they sensed the gift she had or owned a piece of it themselves—or perhaps they simply knew what the herbs were for and assumed that she did, too.

Covering the kitchen table with paper towels, she spread out the tins, wooden boxes, and plastic bags, opening and sniffing the contents of each as she considered its particular power: *angelica*, worn next to the body, could keep away the good as well as the bad; *broom tops*, boiled in salt water, would protect from things that meant one harm; *snakeroot*, good to keep an evil being at bay. She sniffed the *boneset*, also known as *ague weed*, with which one bathed for protection, and set it apart from the others. And then were the herbs used for cooking as well as for protection from accidents in the home: coriander, dill, marjoram.

She opened and sniffed a bag of dried carnation blossoms, the kind Geneva tossed like confetti around the living rooms of each new apartment they moved into, and the anise given to Luna by Geneva for her nightmares (and she'd had plenty of them); their sweet fragrance brought back both the pleasure and pain of her mother's healings. *Pennyroyal*. An ironic smile settled on her lips at the sight. It was used by some as protection from domestic abuse but hadn't done much to protect Geneva. Her father had never laid a hand on her, never uttered a cross word, but his rage at Geneva for her madness and curious ways knew no bounds.

She opened a leather bag of crystals and gemstones. The turquoise pendant she'd given to Jocelyn was a lesser charm offered in the spur of the moment. If she'd had her wits about her, knowing what she knew now, she would have come home and searched for a stronger gem—clear crystal, garnet for its defensive aura; even calcite, broad protection against many woes. She fingered each gem—most attached to silver chains, some to twisted hides.

Blue Tiger's Eye, riddled with navy streaks, was the one her mother had forced her to wear when she'd been a child. It was a heavy pendant, and seeing it, nestled among the others, even now made the base of her neck ache. When she was old enough to escape Geneva's watchful eyes, she'd slip it off, hiding it in her book bag as soon as she left the house, concealing it there until after school, when she was a block from home and she'd dutifully slip it back around her neck once again. She hadn't worn it in years, hadn't needed to.

She laid it aside now, placing it beside the *boneset* as she searched for an oil. *Vetiver*, she decided, with its deep, woodsy odor. To be used, Geneva would tell her, when one entered dangerous surroundings. Geneva had made her wear it to her junior prom, of all things. Lucky for her, it was a pleasantly scented protector—and it *had* kept her tranquil and calm.

The bath was next. She made a tea with *boneset* leaves, adding only a few because they were known both for bitterness and their laxative properties (and *that* would be all she would need). Sipping what she could of the tea, she put the rest of the leaves into a satchel, then dropped them into the tub that she'd filled with warm water. Two candles of equal height—white for protection, black to ward off evil—were quickly lit, and she eased into the warm water. Thankfully, *boneset* had hardly any odor, so she settled into it, comfortably, closing her eyes as she cleared her mind.

When she finished bathing, she dried herself and rubbed the *vetiver* oil on her forehead and wrists, then placed the pendant around her neck, letting it fall freely on her naked breasts. It was one-thirty. An hour until she would leave. Despite the cold, she dressed in a long white cotton dress she'd bought the summer before, then lay down on the bed to gather her thoughts—Pinto settled on her lap as she scratched his ears and back.

Her mind wandered to Jerome, her dead love, and the things they had planned. For the first time in her life she'd dreamt of normalcy, of growing old with someone who knew her frailties. Of Christmas gifts, Thanksgiving turkeys, and a house with sheer white curtains flapping in the windows and red impatiens blooming in the backyard. And of children. How many? Whatever we're blessed with, Jerome would say. But there would be no children for her now. And that made her think about Mikela and the threat Jocelyn, vulnerable and unknowing, had brought into their lives. Wish me luck, she whispered to Pinto and to whatever spirits, living or dead, were listening, and prayed for protection against whatever she might find.

Then it was time to go.

Stopping short, midway to her car, she thought she heard Geneva's voice: You can't do nothing about it. This ain't your fight.

"I'm not going to fight, I'm going to know," she answered,

talking loudly to herself on her drive across town. When she got there, she could see no lights in Jocelyn's house, and she panicked. Was she with him, Luna wondered? What would she say if she confronted them both? Would Jocelyn take his side against her?

It was a clear, cold night and the street was empty; nothing stirred but old newspapers and bits of trash picked up by the wind and discarded. The wind was cold, with a sharp edge, as it blew through the towering firs and oaks, shaking the branches, swirling around the dead brown leaves on the sidewalk. Then suddenly it stopped, and the air was still and filled with expectation, as if waiting for something to happen. She slipped off her down coat so nothing would interfere with the protection of the *boneset*, glanced again at Jocelyn's house and then at the house that awaited her, and got out of the car.

She hadn't really examined his house before, just took in the aura that surrounded it—she'd been too afraid he'd spot her. But now her curiosity got the better of her. She was struck by the size. It was a massive structure, the largest on the block, looming, nearly leaning over Jocelyn's place as if ready to feed. It was built of blackened, cracked brick from another century and had three stories; the white shutters on the top floor were latched, and heavy maroon drapes hung from over the narrow windows in the front; shades were pulled down everywhere else. A tall thick privet hedge, so green it appeared black at night, surrounded the house and yard and would successfully block the view of any curious neighbor.

The front door sat at the end of a long, twisting path of

red and black bricks assembled in an irregular pattern that was uneven in spots. Luna approached it slowly, as if walking in a dream—each step slowly taken, hesitating then beginning again. Twice she tripped on the edge of a brick, catching herself before she fell. When she got to the door, she paused before she rang the doorbell.

What did she expect to find here, how much would he show her? Doubts began to hover and she stepped back. Wouldn't it be better simply to watch from afar, learn more before she approached him?

I don't like the way he looks at my mom. Like somebody who wants something from her, like he wants to hurt us or kill us or something.

Mikela's words reminded her she didn't have a choice, and her courage came back. Once, twice, she rang his bell, wondering who or what would answer as cold fear stirred in the pit of her stomach.

He came smiling and gracious, and the light from the foyer caught the gleam of his silver ring. The half-moon scar on his face made her remember what Caprice had written; she'd forgotten that, as well as how handsome she'd said he was. Foreboding snaked her spine. Stop it, she told herself, touching the amulet inside her blouse. Stop it!

"Luna, isn't it?" So he knew her name. She caught her breath, momentarily charmed by his voice. What is it, she wondered, that she found enchanting? Was it the depth of it, with the seductive lilt meant to captivate, that drew her in, along with his eyes, so deep and black, that gazed into hers as if revealing a secret only she was privileged to hear? He stood back for a second, smiling as if puzzled. "It's a little late for a visit, isn't it? But you're welcome; any friend of Jocelyn's is a friend of mine." He held out his hand as if to take hers, and she drew back instinctively, her fingers clasping the edge of her dress.

"You know who I am?" So he was expecting her.

"Let's say my senses are as well developed as yours."

"I doubt that," Luna said, although she was lying, and she could tell he knew it. What had Jocelyn told him about her? He sensed the boon. Her fears began to get the better of her, and she lifted her wrist to her nose, as if scratching, to sniff the *vertiver*, and its fragrant woodsy scent forced her to be brave.

"It's cold out there, and you without a coat. Are you going to come in and talk or stand on the porch? I'm alone. See for yourself." He stood back, daring her to enter. Where were the others, she wondered? Would they pounce at any moment from nowhere? That woman she'd seen last Saturday night. She had to be the one Caprice had described in her papers. And the boy who dragged his foot. But what of the third, who must have been tucked away somewhere in this house? Were they here all the time, or just when he called them?

She stepped into the foyer and stopped short, recognizing the smell that filled it. *Asafoetida*. Devil's dung. Strange how such a root, as smooth and flavorable as leeks when cooked, smelled so foul when left raw and uncontained. As with most herbs, it could be used for good or ill, depending on the user. Jerome, whose people were Jamaican, on catching a whiff of it under her bed, told her his grandmother spread it on the heads of newborns to prevent ghosts or duppies from entering a child's soul through its fontanel. It was used to protect as well as curse, and said to be a favorite of wolves in certain cultures, and she thought of that now, as she stepped into his lair.

A fire raged in the fireplace, making the room stiflingly hot and uncomfortable. The heat and smell caught in her chest, making it hard to breathe. The room was cloaked in dim light, filled with dark colors—grays, maroons, blacks, reds—absent of light or gaiety. The couch toward which he beckoned encircled the fire like a trap, and she knew that it would swallow her in its comfort, pull away her barriers, if she sat down. The putrid odor permeated the space, but Luna, used to strange and pungent smells, and knowing of its use for good as well as evil, was undisturbed. I can use this as well as he, she thought, closing her eyes and breathing it in. The more she took in, the more powerful she felt. A black cherub on the mantelpiece drew her attention. She imagined tears falling down its tragic face and turned away, unwilling to become its captive.

"Can I get you something to drink—tea, perhaps, or have you had enough of that?" There was a knowing, nasty edge to his voice, petulant and taunting, letting her know he knew about the herb she had drank and why she had drank it. So this would be a game of chess, she thought, each of them anticipating the other's move. She smiled to herself. Lucky that was one of the few things her father's cruelty had taught her—how to plan strategically.

"I've had enough," she said, sure of herself.

"Sit," he ordered playfully, pointing to the couch.

"I prefer to stand."

"An easy getaway?"

"And why would I need that?" She was surprised by the strength in her voice, how easily she mocked him.

"And you are here, why?" He moved forward; she didn't flinch.

"You know as well as I do."

"Your friend, the woman about whom we both care so deeply."

"What do you want from her?"

He smiled a false, wicked grin. "You haven't talked to her recently, have you? If you had, you'd know, because I told her. You are not the friend you claim to be. I offered her my love, everlasting."

"At what price?"

He tilted his head to the side, as if flirting, and moved toward the couch, sinking into it, motioning again for her to join him. "Sit next to me, and I will tell you."

"You're very sure of yourself with women, but I'm not easily seduced."

He chuckled charmingly deep in his throat. "You are a lovely woman, Luna, and I know there was a man who loved you deeply; no doubt there will be more who will enjoy you, but I am tied to only one, who loves me as dearly as I love her."

"Are you so sure?"

"I am." He leaned back on the couch, turning toward her, and Luna found she was drawn into his gaze, hypnotized by it. "Come, sit beside me, and I will tell you about myself . . . and about you."

"Me?" He caught her off guard and her back stiffened.

What could he possibly know about her? Even Jocelyn didn't know the secrets she kept.

"We are two of a kind, Luna. Same rituals held sacred, same fears and ancient gifts; a hindrance in your case, not so much in mine. I knew your gift the moment I saw you. I know who you are, Luna. Come—" He patted the space next to him with a gentleman's courtliness. "I'm not going to hurt you, nor her. I love her. Luna, surely, with your many gifts, you can see that."

"Yes, and my many gifts tell me all I need to know about you—that you are not who you seem, you are not what you pretend to be."

"Think what you will. I don't need your blessing." He turned away from her, his face a mask she couldn't read.

"With my many gifts, I know that there are ways to defeat you," Luna continued, lying and hoping he couldn't tell.

His smile, or what passed for one, was scoffing and condescending. "Ask Jocelyn about me. She will tell you, if you ask. I'm more than I seem . . . and less."

His answer puzzled her. "Less?"

"But let me tell you about yourself. I know that you are jealous of Jocelyn, that you have within you a small, ugly heart that lies and pretends it is good." Luna, startled, shook her head in denial as he continued. "I can see into your core, Luna. I can see into your soul. I'm good at that. I know who you are and the hatred and envy you have for the woman I love—for all she has that you will never have. I know how you long for what she and others like her have, but you are crippled by the thing that holds you. You are as damned as I am. You are cursed and always will be."

"You're wrong." Luna heard the fear in her own voice, the dismay that he had found a hidden corner of her heart.

"A warning to you. Do not make this between us. You don't have power when it comes to beings like me. You know that as well as I do." His voice had lost all charm and held nothing but menace. He had read her lies and smelled her fear.

"I am not like you."

"There is nothing you can do. You are helpless and she will hate you if you try to interfere. She may leave me for a day, a week, or even a month, but in the end she will belong to me forever. Each time we are together, I take a slice of her and she cuts it willingly, lovingly. That's how much power I have over her."

Not even you will ruin this for me! He's taken me places, showed me worlds that you could never understand.

Remembering Jocelyn's last words to her, Luna knew it was the truth.

"What do you think you can do to protect her?" he continued. "Bathe her in oils? Set me on fire? Toss herbal water in my face? Believe me, anything you can think of has been tried time and time again by stronger beings than you. Come on, Luna, you're smarter than that. I am more powerful than anything you hold sacred."

There were noises upstairs: rapid talk between spoiled arguing children, bursts of laughter, and Luna's heart froze because she knew what the sounds were and that they would soon be coming.

"You will not win," she said out of desperation, closing her eyes, wishing it was so.

The smell grew stronger as they crept downstairs. She could hear them on each landing—the clicking of the woman's heels, the dragging foot. He glanced upward, the slightest smile on his full, sensual lips. Luna felt the hair stand on the back of her neck, light and faint, like the tickling of a feather. Cautiously, she watched him, as one does a predator before its killing leap. From the corner of her eye, she saw them enter.

. . . *a hawkish scarred face and a wolfish grin . . . a thin face and eyes that looked older than he.*

So she played the card she'd kept hidden. "Ezra. That is what Caprice called you, isn't it? And if Caprice loved you so, how did she get away? How did you lose her?"

The malice in his eyes stunned her, but she found the voice she thought deserted her and said his name again. "Ezra, Asa, Ezra, Asa, whoever you are, I know that you are from Hell and Jocelyn will, too, because I will tell her."

"I've told her already, you stupid bitch. You're as crazy as your mother."

How did he know? Luna wondered, but she had no time to think. The three had gathered behind him by then, the woman's fingers, long sharp nails resting uneasily on his shoulders, the others waiting, as if for guidance.

There ain't nothing they can do to you to harm you unless you let them in, my baby. They ain't of this world, so there ain't nothing they can do to harm you unless you let them in.

Geneva's voice came, as it always did when she needed it. She'd stopped wondering long ago if her mother knew—in the way only mothers could—that something was bound to do her baby harm. Or perhaps these were her own thoughts, telling her what she already knew.

"And I won't let you in," she said as she stared at each in turn: the woman dressed in the tight-fitting satin dress she had worn when Caprice first saw her; the boy, glancing at his hands; the third, splendid in his suit from long ago. Unchanged and inhuman. And finally her gaze came to rest on him, and he stared back, devouring her body with his eyes, crunching bone and gristle.

Same as beast needs flesh.

"You will never get her," she said calmly. "I am not afraid of you, and Jocelyn loves her life and daughter too much to do what you want her to do."

But his eyes, disdainful and wicked, said nothing would stand in his way—least of all an eleven-year-old girl with her father's quick smile and thick lashes.

Luna made her way to the door, then ran down the long ragged walkway to her car, as a terrible noise that sounded like laughter echoed behind her.

15

to burn inside

Rain pelted Luna's windshield in a steady rhythm as she sat in her car waiting to see Geneva. She shivered uncontrollably and wished she'd taken the time to stop by her apartment to put on something warmer, but Geneva read impressions from clothing, so it was best to go as she was. A thin white dress in the middle of winter might look strange to some people, but style of clothing registered low with the residents in this place, and the staff was too busy doing other things to care one way or the other.

She knew she had to see Geneva before his words, the residue of his essence, left her. Her mixed feelings about the boon and all that it brought had always discouraged her from taking her mother seriously when she rambled on about evil leavings, spirits, and beings who dwelled on living things. She wished now she'd listened.

The heater was turned on full blast but did little to penetrate the chill that seeped into her bones. She took out a Marlboro, smoked it quickly, then lit another. "Damn," she muttered, as much about the fact that she was smoking too much again as about the malice in his eyes and contempt in his voice she knew she could never forget.

It might have killed a person who didn't understand the "unseen" and "unknown," as she'd taken to calling the various aspect of life that, thanks to the boon, inhabited her reality. Most folks would have run home, crawled under the sheets, and gone quietly mad. Not her. Shakespeare sure knew what he was talking about when he'd given Hamlet those lines about more things in heaven and earth than were dreamed of in Horatio's philosophy. There was nothing in heaven, earth, or hell, for that matter, that was beyond her belief. And hell was from where he must have come.

At seven-thirty, Luna rang the doorbell of the home, thankful that they took pity on her and let her inside. Visitors weren't usually allowed until well after breakfast, but they made exceptions for family members. The receptionist said her mother was in the "morning room" that served as a cafeteria, which made Luna smile; it was a good sign. Geneva usually took breakfast, and most of her meals, on a tray in the corner of her room watching anything that played on the small shared television.

The room was larger than expected and surprisingly bright, far more pleasant than the ones where the patients lived. The tables were covered by red-checkered tablecloths, and plants, albeit plastic, hung at the windows. Patients in various stages of dress—robes, nightgowns, and pajamas—sat at the tables or were parked in wheelchairs drawn up to the sides. The smell of bacon and eggs sizzling from grills in the kitchen filled the air, and Luna felt her stomach rumble; despite everything that had happened, she was hungry.

Geneva sat alone at a table in a far corner of the room gazing out of a window, a spoon of Cream of Wheat midway between bowl and mouth. Luna, not wanting to startle her, approached cautiously and stood nearby.

"Been catching demons, ain't you?" she said with a sly smile that made Luna grin.

"How did you know?"

"Could smell him on you. And all that white, I figured you must be up to something showing up here at the crack of dawn. You catch him?" She laid the spoon down carefully on the side of the plate and gazed at her daughter, her piercing eyes focused on Luna, who shook her head. "Didn't I tell you to stay away from that man?"

Luna eased down in the seat beside her mother. Geneva fervently grabbed her hand and kissed her fingertips, sniffing her wrists. "Least you had the good sense to put on that oil." Surprised as always by her mother's actions, Luna watched Geneva cautiously, wondering what she would say or do next, preparing herself for anything. Neither woman spoke. An attendant came and asked Geneva if she wanted to go back to her room; she shook her head. She was one of only a few patients left, and Luna, suspecting he wanted to clear the room to prepare for lunch, assured him she'd take her mother back when she was ready.

A wood-framed door led to a small garden covered by snow and dead leaves. Luna tried to imagine what it might look like in spring, with tulips growing in the rectangular beds or roses climbing up the unpainted trellis. She thought how pleasant it would be to take Geneva there in the summer, sit on one of the benches, breathe in the fragrance of the roses, like a normal mother and daughter talking and laughing together, enjoying each other's company. She closed her eyes as she tried to remember the scent of roses. Geneva glanced at her and shook her head, and then gazed again at the barren garden outside.

"Mama. What do you see?" Luna asked after a minute.

"You can't do nothing. I don't know why you went over there in the first place."

You told me that earlier didn't you? Luna thought and Geneva, as she often did, smiled slightly, knowing exactly what was on her daughter's mind.

"Remember the stuff you read—that belonged to the lady who was dead?" Geneva averted her eyes. "You said a few things, Mama, but you didn't tell me what I needed to know. That's why I went over there. You need to tell me now, or I might need to go back." Geneva glanced up at her daughter, her eyes darting around her eyes and lips.

"You ain't going back there."

"You don't know that," Luna said, knowing very well it did no good to threaten her mother, but also knowing how much her mother loved her, despite her inability to show it.

"Ain't nothing you can do about it even if you knew," Geneva said, glancing down at the empty cup on the edge of her tray. Luna went to a small table at the edge of the room and brought back coffee for herself and tea for Geneva, adding four packets of sugar before she set it down in front of her. She used to worry about how much sugar her mother took in, but it had long since ceased to bother her. Sugar, she realized, was a substitute for liquor, so she poured it into her mother's tea, or even soda occasionally, with no comment. Geneva sipped it slowly, and Luna noticed again the tremor in her hands, how long her nails had grown. She made a mental note to trim them when they got back to the room and check to see if there was any polish left. Geneva had been partial to deep maroon and black long before they became fashionable.

"I need you to tell me everything you know, Mama," she said, sipping her coffee. It wasn't bad, but lukewarm, and she wondered if that was done deliberately to keep trembling hands from burning themselves if it spilled.

"About what?" Geneva said with a coy glance, and Luna, now the impatient parent, shook her head.

"Don't play with me, Mama. Everything."

"Ain't nothing you can do about it. It's her fight to win . . . or lose. Why you care?"

"She's my best friend . . . and there's a child involved," she added, watching her mother closely for her reaction. Geneva loved children—anyone's children.

"He going to hurt a child?"

"He might, if he doesn't get what he wants. Tell me about him."

Geneva pursed her lips, then wrinkled her nose as if she'd picked up a whiff of something foul. "They show up every thirty, sixty years or so to get their fix, what they need to go on living. Like some damn junkie. How long that lady been dead? The one whose story you let me tell?"

"About thirty years. Jocelyn said she was born around the time Caprice died."

"He looking for her then. She must have got away from him to make him desperate like he is. About time for him

211

to show up then, getting what he needs to keep on living and doing the things he do."

"And if he doesn't get it?" Luna had asked Geneva that before and gotten no answer.

"They go on doing whatever he do until the next time, but he'll be weaker then, not able to get what they wants from this old world."

"You keep saying 'them,' Mama."

Geneva glanced sideways at her daughter as if she were trying to fool her.

"They."

"Who are they, Mama?" she asked, knowing very well who her mother was talking about.

"Them that stay around him." Geneva poured more sugar into her tea, watching her daughter out of the corner of her eye.

"You're drinking sugar, Mama, pure cane sugar!" Luna put her hand on her mother's, and Geneva shook it off and grinned.

"Don't you think I know that?" Geneva put her hand over her mouth like a little girl would when she's trying to hold something back, then giggled like a child, which sent Luna into a gale of laughter that felt good because she hadn't realized until then just how much tension was between them, how much they both needed to laugh together, cry, or do anything that bonded them besides the boon.

"You're acting like a kid, Mama, I swear you are."

"You're the child, not me," Geneva said, still smiling. "My child." Tears filled Geneva's eyes, coming from Luna had no idea where, but Luna was silent now, sipping her coffee, waiting for Geneva to open up again.

There was always a risk in pushing Geneva too hard for answers. She'd done that once, and her mother had closed down for weeks, as if sharing what she knew—of worlds that few, if any, others understood—had completely tired her, taking some piece out of her and leaving her speechless. Luna had finally begun to understand her own gift—but was still puzzled by her mother's, which deepened as she aged.

Geneva had told her once that the boon had come to her when she was six, when she first began to hear the voices of the dead: a favorite aunt who died of cancer; a brother dead at birth, who Geneva said still came to her in dreams, talking and joking like a full-grown man. The boon ran through her mother's line, she knew that—passed from mother to child, or so she'd been told. Way back into Africa, she'd told Luna once, when as a girl she'd asked about the strange things she could see around people's heads, the sense she got of things that seemed to come from nowhere.

Luna was grateful her own gifts weren't like those of Geneva, who seemed to know in concrete ways things she could only sense. She wondered about the other women in her mother's family, who except for Polly, her own mother, Geneva rarely mentioned, and how deep their boon went. Would they have known the answers that she sought?

She wondered if they lived life as she did. Better to live life as most people did, happily unaware that there was nothing real outside of what one could see, hear, smell, or hold tight in a hand. Ignorance was, indeed, the truest bliss.

"He calls them when he needs them, to do his bidding. They ain't nothing without him. But he needs them like they do him. They get their evil from him, but they lesser beings who won't survive without him, and they know it same as him. He takes them with him. If he die, so do they, so they do what he say. Make it easier for him to do his nastiness."

"Are they alive?"

"What you think?" Geneva snapped, shaking her head at her daughter's ignorance. "They soulless, same as him. He collect them, make them promises, then eat them alive."

"Then he's a demon?"

"Demon, incubus; they used to call them that, too, in the old times. They don't call them much of nothing now, but I know what he is; he don't change. He takes what he can get from those who don't know he wants it. What he look like?"

"Handsome. Like Caprice said in her writing," Luna said, watching for Geneva's response.

"Incubus. The ones who want the women always are—good-looking like that. The ones who want the men are prettier than you could ever think. Succubus, that's what they called. That's what he sound like to me, but there's all kinds of blendings of evil, ain't just one thing or the other."

"Where do they come from?"

Geneva shrugged her shoulders. "Always been here, I guess. Right from the beginning. Sumeria. Mesopotamia. He probably wasn't here as long as that, but something of him was. Different places, too. Europe. Brazil right down in that rainforest. In Brazil, they say they dump the women in the river, that's what Polly used to tell me, and she knew just about everything there was to know about them kinds of things."

"But how did Polly know these things, Mama?" She'd asked that question so many times. According to Geneva, Polly was the source of all knowledge.

"Just did. I've told you that since you were six. I wish I knew, but I don't."

Luna felt like a cigarette; her mother shook her head. "Now you know how I feel when I need that drink." She grinned good-naturedly.

"It's not the same, Mama."

"You don't think so?" Geneva threw back her head and laughed, drawing the attention of several residents at other tables. "Go on and get one then. They let you outside if you want to go."

"Will you come with me?"

"Too cold out there for me."

Luna stepped outside, the cold wind ripping through her thin cotton dress. She lit a cigarette, inhaling deeply, and decided that maybe Geneva was right: addiction was addiction. She glanced at her mother through the glass door. Geneva gazed out the window, her thoughts clearly not on her daughter, shivering in the cold, but somewhere distant, that place where they had always gone for as long as Luna could remember.

Would she be like that someday, Luna wondered, her mind drifting places where nobody else's could go? What use would she be to anyone then? And who would visit her when her mind was finally gone and all she had left was the boon telling her things she didn't want to hear? Stomping the cigarette into the dirt, she stepped back in, bringing the cold air with her, and Geneva focused on her daughter, a stricken look on her face.

"Did he touch you?" she asked, her voice quivering. The panic in her mother's voice alarmed her. For a moment she thought Geneva was asking about sex in some old-fashioned, courtly way, then realized she literally meant "touch."

"Why?"

"Tell me!"

"No, he didn't," Luna said, quickly reassuring her, thinking back to that moment when she'd first come into the house, and the sharp memory of the smell of devils' dung and how the colors in the room unsettled her. Something had made her draw back, unwilling to feel his hand upon her own. "What happens if he does?"

"His skin must touch yours for him to burn inside you. That's how he gets his hold. Touching your hand with his, his lips on yours, body pushing its way inside you.

"It's blood for some, binding them into your life. Trading your life for theirs. Fear for others, scaring you half to death with their evil until you damn near lose your mind—but touch for those who prey on women like your friend, who don't know no better. Asleep to their power. Then he gets what he really come for—the essence of her being."

"Was the first one weak? Caprice?"

Geneva shook her head. "He wouldn't be back if she'd given him what he wanted. She must have been stronger than he thought, so he come back for a second try."

"Then Caprice escaped him?"

"And he come back to get her again."

"But Jocelyn is growing stronger. She has her weak moments like everybody else, but she's tougher than she looks," Luna said, defending her friend even as she remembered Jocelyn's insecurities.

"You don't know nothing, do you?" Geneva said with a dismissive shrug. "They see inside you. They know who they can get and can't."

"He is evil, then?"

"Wasn't always that way. Probably wishes he wasn't, but he's been too long that way to change. They do sometimes, though." Geneva sipped her tea, leisurely enjoying it, adding packets of sugar as her daughter watched.

"It's all sugar now, Mama, there's no tea left. Just sugar!"

"That's all I need, sugar. That's what your daddy used to call me, do you remember that, my baby? He used to call me Sugar."

"And other things," Luna said bitterly. The memories of the other names came flooding back: crazy bitch, devil's fool—dumbass loony, in lighter moments. "Don't make him more than he was."

"Humph. I'm here. He ain't. That should tell you something." Luna chuckled because Geneva was right. She had outlived him and had the last word. "Did he touch you?" Her mother peered at her, asking again.

"I told you, no!"

"But something happened, I know that just from looking at you."

Luna dropped her head, unable to look into her mother's face. Geneva reached across the table, took her daughter's hand, and Luna felt her eyes fill with tears.

"I'm scared, Mama."

"What you got to be scared of?"

"He knows about you, he knows who you are."

Geneva chuckled. "I been around long enough to know how to deal with evil like that—for myself anyway, not for the girl. What else?"

"He told me he could see into my soul," Luna said, whispering. "He said I was jealous of Jocelyn, hated her . . . he said my heart was small and evil . . ."

"He told you that to scare you, same as why he mentioned me."

"But was it the truth?"

"You got a big heart, baby, you always have. You know that as well as me, but what else you expect a demon to say? He a demon, ain't he?" Geneva shook her head in exasperation, and Luna erupted in a burst of laughter at the wisdom of her mother's words. Geneva joined in, both laughing heartily at the ironic truth nobody else could understand. "But you put that oil on, didn't you?" Geneva's eyes turned serious.

"That and everything else you tried to teach me." *Taught me*, Luna thought. Despite what she often told herself, her mother's lessons had embedded themselves inside her.

"You did all you could do then, Luna. The battle is hers, not yours."

"But what about the child?" Luna asked, the thought of Mikela sobering her, making her afraid.

"The child ain't yours. It's her choice to make. She give that baby life, and she the one who going to take it away."

"She'll never hurt Mikela."

"If he tell her to, she will. He'll make her kill it if it serves him. Sure as I breathe air, he'll chase her down until she kills it, unless she gets him first."

"And how does she do that? Get him first?"

"If she's lucky, she'll know what to call on inside her when the time comes. If not, well, I guess that baby's dead sure as she'll be along with her sorry soul."

"Mama, there must be something else. Something she can do." Desperation swept Luna, along with anguish at her helplessness.

"Get me some more tea and I'll think on it."

Luna dutifully filled her mother's cup with hot water and a Lipton tea bag, tossing in two bags of Splenda to cut back on the sugar. She brought it to the table, and Geneva took a sip and shook her head.

"Don't you think I know sugar when I taste it?" Geneva gave the cup back to her daughter.

"You can't blame me for trying."

"Sometimes folk say there's something that will draw them to you. Something that belonged to the spirit they looking for, that's calling to his evil. Fire will clean anything. Blood, flesh, bone. Won't kill him but might get rid of him for a bit, long enough for him to leave her alone. Tell her to burn whatever belonged to the lady who brought him, the one who wrote the papers."

"That's all?" Luna asked, clearly disappointed.

"That's all I know, what Polly used to tell me," Geneva said with a helpless shrug, and Luna knew it was time to take her back to her room. Hand in hand, the two walked back to the room where Geneva felt safe, and she let her head fall on her daughter's sturdy shoulder.

16

what of you is true?

It was Sunday. Four weeks had passed since Jocelyn had seen him. The first week she lay in bed, not answering the phone or door because she knew it was him calling. The second week she watched endless reruns of *Law & Order*, and he sent roses—blood red same as always—and she left them packed in their box on the dining room table. She did, however, read the note (there seemed no risk in that) apologizing for whatever he had done to frighten her. She promptly threw the note away. But the scent of the roses lingering in the room made her drunk with thoughts of him, until she stuffed them into a black plastic trash bag and threw them outside in a garbage can far down the street.

By the third week, she was still afraid, fearful he would call and the sound of his voice would bring her to him. But when she got out of bed, played back the messages, and heard his voice—the begging, the rage—she hardened her heart, remembering what he had said that last time they had been together and knowing that nothing could draw her back.

He was crazy, she decided. The drugs, the hard living, the sorrow at the loss of those kids—even though he claimed they weren't his—had made him lose his mind, and he might have taken her right along with him if she'd let him. Her own sanity had been at risk.

If he wasn't clinically insane, he was close. Maybe this latest thing was one of the crazy games he liked to play. He loved doing that, like with the blindfolds, velvet bindings, him swearing he was—and becoming—someone or something she feared—the thing that pawed at her heart, as he once suggested. It was thrilling at first, the fearful anticipation of what he would do next—what craziness would occur to him. But then it became frightening. He knew enough about her fears to play on them and scare her. He would stop when she begged him to, but only moments before she reached her breaking point, when her heart was beating so fast she was certain she would die.

The whole thing could have been part of some game he was playing, with her imagination taking over, the drugs playing their part, too. The scar? Coincidence. Or maybe she'd shared what she'd read in Caprice's writings about the man Caprice was involved with and he'd taken them and used them against her. She'd gotten so high with him so many damn times she could barely recall what she did or didn't tell him. Had the scar even been there in the beginning? So much was blurred by time and dope she couldn't remember.

He was right about that night, though. She *had* imagined it all. Proof had come when those very people appeared in familiar places. Why, just the other day in Whole

Foods, the apricot-colored woman had been standing at the register prepared to ring up her order. Jocelyn had been startled by the sight of her and switched to another line, realizing as she did so how foolish she must have seemed, and when she looked up, the woman was gone. Probably on break.

Obviously, she had seen the woman before in the store, taken her into her memory, and imagined she saw her standing behind Asa in his house that night. She was seeing things that were never there—like the boy with the limp mowing the neighbor's lawn the other morning; he dropped his head when she looked in his direction. Courteous boy, polite. And the other, the evil one—she saw him cutting hedges down the street. You see what you want to see or are afraid of seeing. They vaguely resembled characters she'd read about in Caprice's papers—innocent victims who became actors in her deranged drama.

She was almost as crazy as he was!

The day before, she had begun returning Mike and Luna's calls, apologizing for not getting back to them sooner, explaining she'd needed space, had to find a way back into her life. With some trepidation, each asked if she was still seeing—as Mike put it—the rich guy with the silver car, and she told them that she wasn't, that they had broken up.

On the phone with Mike, she could hear the relief in his voice. She explained that she needed to clean the house before he brought Mikela back, and she would need about a week to do it. He told her he'd call her then, and they'd make plans from there.

"Can I talk to Mikela?" she asked him.

He hesitated. "I don't know."

"Please, Mike."

"I'll ask her."

Jocelyn held her breath waiting for Mikela's voice, and when she heard it, she couldn't find her own.

"Mom, are you there?" The panic in Mikela's voice broke Jocelyn's heart.

"I am, honey," she managed to say. "I will be from now on. I just want you to know how much I love you, and that . . . I'm okay now."

Silence on the other end.

"Mikela?"

"Yeah."

"Please forgive me."

"Okay," Mikela answered in a small, hesitant voice.

She wept for a while after that, and then called Luna.

"So what happened?" Luna demanded to know.

"Listen, girl, I don't want to go into it now, it's too outrageous. I'll tell you when I see you. It was just weird, that's all."

"Weird? Tell me."

"I don't know, Luna, Just weird." She could barely believe the things he had said to her. How could she expect her friend to understand or accept them? "He just said some wild-ass stuff that made me . . . well . . . kind of freaked me out. I'm okay now."

"When you told him you were breaking up with him, did you wear that pendant I gave you?"

"The necklace?" Jocelyn had forgotten all about it. Panicked, she glanced at the hook in her closet where she'd put it to make sure it was still there. "You mean the turquoise and silver one? I'll give it back when I see you. And I didn't exactly tell him—I just left," she said, avoiding the question about the pendant.

"You didn't wear it then."

"No, no, I didn't."

"You haven't seen him since?"

"I haven't seen him, and I don't want to see him. It's definitely over."

Luna paused before she spoke. "Do you have anything that belongs to your great-grandmother?"

"Huh? Like what?"

"Anything. Clothing, jewelry. Something that has been passed down that belonged to her."

"I don't think so. They were both so mad at her, anything she passed on they probably threw away. There are just the papers she wrote, the ones like I gave you."

"Nothing else?"

"No, I don't think so. What does that have to do with anything?"

"And you're sure it's over?"

"With Asa? Yeah." Jocelyn was amused at Luna's persistence. "And anyway, he's gone. Out of the country. I'm pretty sure about that."

"Don't be too sure. Call me if you need me. If you see him again."

"Okay, Luna," Jocelyn said, chuckling to herself. At least, Luna hadn't changed.

"Promise me?"

"Okay, I promise." After all, Luna had been right about the guy, but for all the wrong reasons. It was funny how her lust and loneliness had put brakes on common sense.

But it was over. She hadn't heard from him since the flowers, and his car was gone. The shades in the house were drawn and nothing moved. He must be traveling again, like she'd told Luna. He did that whenever he got down. Hadn't he told her, the first time he met her, that he spent most of his time traveling the world? Madrid, New Orleans, Cairo—he could go anywhere he wanted to. Why the hell would he stay in Jersey?

Asa would always be a mystery to her. There were things one couldn't explain in life, and he was certainly one of them. In the meantime, she would put him out of her mind, forget the sex, the love—or whatever the hell it had been.

When she'd run from him that Monday morning, chased by his words and the fear he unleashed, she'd slammed the door, locking it behind her. It was only after she'd called Mike and talked for those few brief moments that she felt at home again, as if she'd stepped back into a safe, stable space she'd forgotten. As she looked around the house now, she noticed to her dismay the state of that space.

Pig sty! Mikela was right, that was just what it had become. What would Constance or Nana France say if they saw it? She opened windows, letting in the cool, fresh air, and began to clean, working up a sweat, throwing herself into basic, concrete tasks: scouring, sponging, dusting, polishing. Several of the dishes were so soiled with dried food they had to be thrown away. Cabinets, stove surfaces, spoiled leftovers in the refrigerator and on the floor—everything she touched, everywhere she stepped was dirty. Inch by inch, piece by piece, she scrubbed and washed, throwing muscle and will into her work, purging mind and body.

She soaped the kitchen until it smelled like pine; it was mindless work that she usually hated, but she needed it now to take her thoughts off him—how much she still missed him, how much, to her disgust, she had loved him. And as she cleaned, his words came back to haunt her:

I can never let you go. Not again. It's beyond that now.

Again! To let her go again.

You need to know who I am . . . what I am.

So just what are you, Asa? A fucking crazy man? A fucking deranged asshole? That's what you are? Someone who will drive me as nutty as you with whatever spell you had on me, whatever drug you had me on. I guess the Markham women's curse is on me, too, you son of a bitch!

She yelled out loud, as if confronting him, realizing as she raised her voice that she'd rarely done it when she was with him, had never challenged him.

And what if I told you I was that man? The man your great-grandmother loved.

That angered her more than anything, using her great-grandmother's memory to keep her, using her family in whatever crazy game he was playing. How could he have known the things he seemed to know? She *must* have told him. When did she tell him so much? Why had she done it?

Marimba's children were not mine. They belonged to Marimba.

Why did you lie about that?

To convince you to stay.

Because you knew your story would touch me?

227

How else could I get you to love me?

He preyed on her goodness, and she'd been so lonely and stupid she'd let him do it—believed anything, no questions asked.

What of you is true?

It said more about her than it did him, and that made her feel ashamed and foolish.

As foolish as Caprice.

And I am not Caprice, she said to Nana France, Constance, and finally to Asa himself, runner of cruel, deceptive games.

There can be nothing left of you but me. That is my condition.

Recalling those words, spoken with such coldness and indifference as if he knew she would give him what he wanted, frightened her more now even than before. Had she been on the verge of giving it? When he first made that crack about Mikela, about bringing her back when they needed her, was that what he had been talking about?

I will put this out of my mind, she said, scrubbing the inside of the oven (forgetting it was self-cleaning). I will put you out of my mind forever!

She started in the morning and worked until midnight, falling into bed when she was too tired to think or lift her arms. At seven the next morning, she was up again and came down to her sparkling, lemon-smelling kitchen, dialed her radio to a salsa station that made her want to dance, and made oatmeal and coffee, the only edible things she could find in her cupboards. I'll cook for Mikela when Mike brings her over, she decided—chicken and dumplings, she'd always loved that, and Mike will stay because he loves them, too. That made her feel good, to consider something as mundane as shopping and cooking.

Bucket in hand, she headed upstairs to the bedrooms, pulling damp towels and moldy washcloths off racks, stripping wrinkled sheets and blankets off beds, hauling the plastic bags filled with dirty clothes downstairs to the basement to wash and dry them. She glanced toward the attic. Was it time now to take on that daunting task, the one her mother had begun? Soon, she decided. Very soon.

As she headed into her bathroom, a whiff of lemon verbena soap made her remember the last time she saw him, and she stopped mid-step, feeling anger, then sorrow, and finally a sharp sense of loss that caught her unprepared. How had he bewitched her so completely? If only he had actually been the man she'd thought he was—charming, thoughtful, erudite. If only she had left when his tenderness turned malevolent. If only he hadn't been so fucking crazy!

The phone rang, and she caught her breath, wondering if by simply thinking about him she'd called him to her. She let it ring—five, six times—waiting for the message machine to come on with a recorded message.

It was Laura from the library:

Hope you're feeling better and that you're coming in next week back on schedule. And don't forget those papers. We're going to do a joint venture with one of the other branches. See you then.

Quick and to the point. Jocelyn could hear her annoyance and was grateful she still had a job. Laura was good about giving time off to deal with "family issues," and after that loudmouthed fight she'd had with Mike in the middle of the library, she saw what was going on. But Jocelyn knew she had to get back in Laura's good graces.

She'd nearly forgotten her promise to finish Caprice's papers. After Asa's craziness, she'd put them aside until she was feeling stronger. But Laura had mentioned them to a librarian at another branch, and she'd be furious—and embarrassed—if Jocelyn let her down. There weren't many pages left; she could go through them later tonight, remove the ones that revealed too much, then take the rest to the library later in the week.

She had tomato soup and a tuna fish sandwich for dinner, rewarding herself with the last of some Häagen-Dazs rum raisin ice cream she found packed in the back of the freezer. There was a load of sheets in the dryer. She took out her mother's favorite set and folded them, still warm and fragrant, to put on her bed that night. She made a cup of chamomile tea, which reminded her of Luna, so she called her, and when there was no answer, she sent her a text asking that she drop off Caprice's papers as soon as she could. Jocelyn smiled to herself when she thought about her friend; it would be good to see Luna again. Then she went upstairs. Pulling the well-worn parcel out of her bureau drawer, she settled down on the edge of her bed and began to read.

17

a haven of mercy

*It went on for years, it seemed. I begged him to let me
go, to allow me to leave him, but he refused. What was
he waiting for? I was unsure at first. He kept up his talk
about sending for you, allowing me to see you, which was
a change from what he'd said before and the rage that
would meet the mention of your name, so I was wary.*

I grew to hate him.

*There were smiles and gentle courtesies when we were
around others, which was seldom, and other gifts—black
pearls from the South Seas, roses thrown on our bed
in red profusion—but they grew repugnant. I was
suspicious of all flowers because of the opium that would
make me forget, seduce me into loving him, bring me the
peace I craved.*

*It was an adventure at first: Mott Street with its
brilliance and color—red and gold mostly, the colors of
wealth and good luck. People swarmed there from all
over the world in clothing unknown to me: pajamas of
fine silk and black cotton, starched tuxedos, exquisite*

saris and kimonos that flowed over graceful, exotic women. The streets held the same excitement touched with expectation that I found in Harlem—but there was a slower rhythm, a different syncopation.

The nights were brightly lit bazaars overflowing with knickknacks both dear and of no value—porcelain vases and urns, flimsy paper lanterns, pearls and black coral necklaces, exquisitely carved jade earrings that hung nearly to one's chin. But the alleys were dark and menacing, and that was where we would find the flower houses, their fragrance floating into the street, enticing and seductive.

The fumes were sweet and delicious, and when I fell back on the silken cushions, sucking in the vapors through the long elegant pipes—jade for me, ivory for him—I was pulled into the nothingness that he claimed was much like death. We'd return home laden with prizes: special pipes and lamps to burn the black, sticky tar, and soon there was no need to travel back. I could stay in our place, overtaken by it. He would come and go as he pleased; I no longer cared.

It was only by chance I discovered the letter he sent to my sister Clementine. It had been returned unopened with the address unknown. What did he want from her, I wondered? Why had he not told me? The seal was broken, so I was able to read the first lines. He requested that she send you North, to live with me, because you were needed by your mother. I knew nothing of this because I had long since decided you were better off with her, as far away from me as you could get.

And why did he want you here when so often he refused? He knew that I still loved you. All of me, he wanted, even that part that belonged to you, which he could never have so he had to kill it.

The seasons came and went, but I took no notice. I would wake, stay in bed until he came to me, and after that we would smoke. I had become a shadow of myself. I was thin, and my skin had lost its luster. I no longer looked in the mirror for fear of what I would see. Hair came out in bunches. I bathed but there was no pleasure in it. All that I cared about was to flee into my mind, to feel nothing, and I realized that perhaps he was right: I had died already, so why not give him what he wanted most?

It would be quick, he'd told me, and I would be with him always. Like stepping through a door, he said, into a place that I would never leave. To take what was most precious to me and give it to him for our love. To cut my ties with everything mortal.

How long had we been together, he and I?

How much time had passed before the woman came?

He had gone out on business that day—something had come up, I remembered him telling me, somewhere in the haze of the opium. She came in uninvited without the others. From upstairs, I guessed. I had finally figured out who they were and where they lived. They never came when he was absent, and I was afraid at first, as she sat and watched me, catlike and secretive, her weary, empty eyes studying me. I was dressed in his blue silk dressing gown, my hair undone, my face unwashed. Had she come to laugh at me, I wondered? I remembered the scorn I'd seen in her eyes at Madame Queen's.

Was it jealousy, I wondered, or simply pity? I lay on his bed, holding my jade pipe. A beautiful thing it was, intricately carved and so heavy I could barely hold it. He held it for me when he was there, telling me how much he loved me, how much he needed me with him.

"Ezra is not here," I said, the smell of the tar sweet and overpowering as I sucked it in, losing myself in its magic, my eyes closed, head rocking forward then back. Gently, she took the pipe from my lips, bent close to me, whispered in my ear.

"Run, now this moment, or he will do to you what he has done to me."

This was the first time I had heard her voice, a low rumble, words slurred as if she was drunk, fear in her voice and eyes. She drew a gold locket from her ample bosom and pressed it into my palm, disappearing as silently and quickly as she had come.

Something took hold of me then. I pulled myself up, dressed quickly. I'd bought a carpetbag a few weeks before in Chinatown and now I stuffed it with things easily carried—jewelry that could be traded for cash, the handkerchiefs I had embroidered for you, the Chanel perfume I so loved. Stacks of cash were hidden in a drawer in his oak desk, and I shoveled the bills into the bag, not bothering to count them. I pulled on one of my coats, mink with fox trim, planning to sell it in the spring.

I made my way quickly out of his building, speaking

to no one. *Luck was with me. I found a cab, took it
downtown, switched to another, and then to Grand
Central Station, in case he traced the two. I boarded the
first train leaving, going anywhere—north or south. It
was headed to Providence, Rhode Island, and that,
indeed, became my providence.*

*On the outskirts of that small city, I found a
boarding house that welcomed colored women. I have
always been lucky with landladies, and the one who ran
this one knew a jeweler who gave me fair money for my
jewels, no questions asked. All I kept was the locket,
although it was solid gold and would have brought a
good price. The initial "M" was engraved on its surface,
but when I pried open the heart I found nothing but two
empty halves. What had become of those she held
precious?*

*It took a month to rid myself of the opium inside me,
though I craved it nearly every day. After its hold was
loosened, I found employment as a maid and seamstress
to Miss Lena Simmons, a wealthy elderly woman who
valued my learning. I served her faithfully until she died,
then lived with her younger sister, Ida, a charitable
spinster committed to those less fortunate.*

*For several years, I lived in fear of him finding me,
rarely leaving the Simmons home. Finally, I gathered the
courage to write to my younger brother, just a boy when
I'd left, begging for information about you. He gave me
Clementine's address in Philadelphia. With money I'd
saved, I set out to see you. When I arrived at the address,
Clementine told me you were in school. She was as*

unforgiving as she was protective, and forbade me to
see you. But she promised she would write to keep me
abreast of noteworthy events in your life. I decided this
was for the best. I still feared he would find me and drive
me to do us both harm.

Clementine kept her promise. As the years passed,
she told me of your well-being and achievements. When
you graduated from high school and college she sent me
the programs. There was a copy of the newspaper notice
when you married your smart young lawyer, and a photo
of the house you bought a few years later. I was sixty
when your first child was born and determined to see you
and my only grandchild. Clementine was dead by then.

I know you will never forget that brief visit, nor will I.
Unsure of my reception, I asked the cab to wait outside.
I rang your bell, stepped inside to greet you, and there
you were—everything I had hoped for in a daughter—so
beautiful and strong, confident and sure, but wary of me.
You named your daughter Constance, someone constant
in your life, and I held her to my breast for one sweet,
blessed moment. Her name was a good one, because I
disappeared again, this time forever.

I will tell you now why I fled without a backward
glance, saying nothing, not even good-bye. As you
remember, you invited me to spend the night, and I
returned to the cab to collect my suitcases, leaving my
bag upon your porch. It was then that I heard his voice.

He called my name, and I stopped, unbelieving,
turning to look at him once again. He was unchanged.
Not a wrinkle on his handsome face nor gray hair on his

head. There was no stoop in his walk or hesitancy in the charming smile that came so easily. He reached toward me, nearly touching me, and I fled back to the cab and to Providence and safety as quickly as I could.

I took refuge in a women's place of protection, the Haven of Mercy, supported by the Simmons sisters, and lived there in solitude and fear, preparing meals, cleaning, ironing, looking out for young souls as lost as I had been. I will die here, I am sure of that, but death will be welcomed on my own terms in its own manner.

These last years have passed more slowly than I thought possible—each one far longer than the day before it. Yet I count each hour a blessing because I saw your face before I died and have been spared another glance at his.

ASA

Who are you to question what my love demands? I know the depth of love and the power of its evil. I know the heights it brings to those who celebrate its power. I will follow you for generations if it takes that long to claim you as my own, for you to give me what I need. I loved you more deeply than I loved even her, and yet you turned your back on me, condemned me to live in this Netherland of lost souls. Caprice, I promise you this: I will allow you no peace as long as there is earth, heaven, and hell until I can possess you until the end of all time.

18

gifts that remained

Jocelyn read the pages twice before she put them down, overcome with sorrow for Caprice—and for her daughter. Nana France had been wounded by her mother in ways she would never understand and expressed that pain in angry, bitter ways. And her only child, Constance, *would* always be a constant presence in her life.

Thank you, dear compassionate ladies, for making my last days on this Earth as peaceful as they could be and for delivering this, what remains of my life, to where it must go.

May she live in peace, away from the turmoil I have brought on myself, and take what is strong from me and destroy what remains.

These final pages, the last testament to her great-grandmother's life, must have been mailed to Nana France by the "compassionate ladies" of the Haven of Mercy shelter, supported so long by Constance with no explanation. Nana France must have received them soon after Caprice's death, then stuffed them away in the attic without a second glance. She had stayed as angry at her absent mother, as unforgiving, as Aunt Clementine, the woman who'd raised her.

She had shown up on the porch, a frightened shabby old woman with rotting teeth and a filthy carpetbag, and disappeared again without saying good-bye.

Nana France's words, not Constance's, but passed on like so many other memories of her "capricious" "foolish" mother. As for the man who had shown up with neither a "wrinkle on his handsome face nor gray hair on his head," he must have been imagined. Some stranger passing on the street who bore a resemblance to the man from whom she'd run. And "he"? Long dead, more than likely. At the thought of him, Jocelyn shook her head in disgust.

Caprice's papers had been tucked away so long ago, yet Constance must have copied them so painstakingly (lovingly?). Mikela had called it right: It *was* like something Grandma might do. Yet why had Constance never mentioned it? Perhaps she had brought them to the basement to go through before she shared them. She may have planned on mentioning them but never had the chance; death had been too swift and unexpected. Tears came to Jocelyn's eyes. There were so many questions she'd meant to ask her mother, so many things that would never be explained.

May she live in peace away from the turmoil that I have brought on myself and take what is strong from me and destroy what remains.

What had Caprice meant by those words?

What else had Constance discovered? There must be other things she'd found and not mentioned. It was late, but Caprice's last pages had piqued her curiosity, and Jocelyn knew sleep would be impossible until she checked the attic to see what else she could find.

When she was a child, the attic had been the one place in the house she avoided. Family treasures and junk that Nana France and Constance were unwilling or unable to part with invariably found their way there. It was dark and eerie, filled with spectral shapes jutting unexpectedly from corners and crevices. Spiderwebs hung willowy and undisturbed; field mice scampered into corners when the light went on. Nana France, fearful of rats, had had rat poison put down several times, but nothing was ever thrown away.

Jocelyn made her way up the winding stairs to the attic, hesitating before she opened the door, groaning at the meager light shed by the single light bulb, and waited for the mice to scamper back to where they'd come from. The room was damp, smelling of mothballs, mold, and—was she imagining it?—a hint of Chanel, which made her smile when she thought of the women—her mother and Caprice—who had loved it. She understood now why it was her mother's favorite perfume, homage to a dead, misunderstood grandmother who had held her for one sweet moment and never returned.

Boxes filled with old toys and discarded artificial Christmas trees were strewn around the room. Two old steamer trunks were parked near the back of the room, next to an oak wardrobe that bulged with men's old-fashioned clothes and shoes that had once belonged to someone—father, grandfather, old boyfriend? Jocelyn grabbed the sleeve of a white linen jacket and shook it, dust filling her nose and mouth, recalling in that instant the birthday dream she'd had about her father that night—so loving and all dressed in white. Had she seen him in this jacket and it tucked its way into her mind? But how could that be; he'd died before she began crawling? Had Constance been unable to throw it away?

Stacks of discarded shoe boxes in one corner were filled with broken costume jewelry. She headed toward them, knocking over a dilapidated dollhouse that she'd treasured as a child. Next to that were stacked boxes neatly labeled with names. Constance, always a master of organization, had clearly been through here. Jocelyn spotted her name neatly printed on a torn cardboard box and eagerly went through it, discovering ancient Barbie dolls, My Little Ponys, and Play-Doh molds hard as bricks. She pulled out an old silk robe once worn by Constance and a black beret sported by Nana France during her flirtation with (and brief financial support of) the Black Panthers during the sixties. Mildewed children's books—*Goodnight Moon*, *The Velveteen Rabbit*, *Where the Wild Things Are*—read by Constance, and later by Jocelyn to Mikela, were randomly scattered. Jocelyn marveled again at how little she had known her mother. Constance, who she had always deemed the mistress of anti-clutter, had kept bits of all their histories.

Nana France's boxes sat behind hers. Coughing from dust, Jocelyn dragged them out in the open, leaving behind a trail of dirt on the bare wooden floor. A spot of silver caught her eye. Nana France's silver lighter lay on a collection of scratched Dinah Washington 45s atop a ratty fox stole with beady eyes and tiny sharp teeth that had terrified her as a child.

She picked up the lighter, running her fingers over the

embossed roses. She clicked it and a tiny blue flame flickered, struggled to stay alive, then died. The memory of Nana France, coffee or gin always in hand, sipping and blowing out smoke rings made her laugh out loud. Nana France, always on her side. She dropped the lighter deep into the pocket of her jeans so she wouldn't forget to take it downstairs.

A whiff of Chanel came from the other side of the room, and for a moment she couldn't move. Something of Constance must be here as well. Or was it her imagination again? Would it stay with her forever, this anguish over her mother's death?

Something caught the corner of her eye, and she went to investigate. It was the weathered leather strap of an old carpetbag tucked behind the oak closet in the back of the attic. The strap looked as if it had been violently ripped from the bag, standing up as if to grab her attention. Knocking aside an old tricycle packed in a box of deflated beach balls, she grabbed the satchel, pulling hard to dislodge it from its hiding place.

It had been beautiful once, its fabric the weight of an Oriental rug, but the color of the ornate design had faded long ago. She decided it must have been maroon with blue swirls and arabesques, and she felt a bond with it she hadn't expected to feel. Caprice loved you so much, she whispered to Nana France, touching the bag as if it had life. You could never forgive her, but I can.

Take what is strong from me and destroy what remains.

Why had those words come to her so abruptly?

The bag was too heavy to carry downstairs. Hesitant to trust the battered straps, she dragged it into an open space underneath the light bulb to unhook the clasp that rust and moisture had tightly sealed. She tried to pry it open, gently and then with force, but it was of no use; she would need to get something stronger, and try it again in brighter light to see what she was doing.

And she was tired. It had been a day of discovery, and this final revelation, as sweet as it was, would have to wait until morning when daylight could filter in through the tiny attic window.

"Tomorrow," she whispered to herself, with a nod at the the carpetbag as she closed the attic door. Slipping off her jeans and sweater, she showered away the attic dust, then dropped down exhausted into bed. Sleep came quickly and violently, bringing a dream within a dream.

First came the smell, unidentifiable, then recognizable as it slipped inside the room. It crept underneath her skin, and she tried not to breathe it in, but it became part of her. It had come with him and she knew he was here, in her room, her mother's room. His weight crushed her, his breath was hot and heavy in her ear. He whispered a name she'd never heard before, then grabbed her breasts, his fingers parting her thighs. No! she screamed, and tried to shake him off, but she could feel him scratching his way into her heart, his hands sharp, hanging like claws. He tore her lips with his crooked teeth, forcing his tongue, rough and slender like a snake, into her mouth, down her throat, and she gagged as it stroked inside her, possessing her. As hard as death, he pushed his way inside her, and she screamed his name to stop him, but he slapped her once, twice until her skin tore like paper into a half-moon mark upon her cheek.

Watching them, perched upon a high-backed chair beside the bed, sorrowful eyes pensive and empty, sat the apricot-colored woman, long black hair hanging down her back, murmuring words Jocelyn couldn't understand. The others were there, too, the boy with his lame foot, hitting the side of the wall, the wolfish one, eyes filled with hatred.

She awoke to darkness. In a circle of light in the middle of the room sat Mikela, throat cut deep, blood oozing out. Jocelyn screamed her daughter's name, reached out to her, tried to close the wound, but still it gaped. Mikela, thick eyelashes clotted with blood, trembled as she died.

His words came clear and strong:

I can see into your soul, Jocelyn. You are as tied to me as I am to you. There is nowhere that you can go that I will not be with you.

"No!" Jocelyn screamed. "No! No! No!"

She opened her eyes. Daylight was outside her window. But the smell was still there, faint, almost as thin as the Chanel that randomly came and went. She buried her head under the sheet, closing her eyes. Was she awake or dreaming? Had she imagined what she'd seen or had he been here?

The phone rang and then the doorbell. Was it him? She pulled herself out of bed, peeked at his house. The shades were still drawn, his car nowhere to be seen. The morning sun brought her back to herself, and when the phone rang a second time, she picked it up cautiously, still shaken.

"Mom, you left the screen door locked so I couldn't get in. We're outside," said Mikela. Jocelyn pulled her jeans off the floor, slipped into them, pulled on her sweater and tore down the stairs into the kitchen. She opened the door and grabbed Mikela, holding her tightly, burying her face in her daughter's hair. She couldn't get enough of the feel and smell of her child.

"Mom, come on, let me go!" Embarrassed, Mikela tried to wiggle out of her arms.

"Not yet!" Jocelyn whispered.

"Mom, stop it!" Mikela said, but Jocelyn knew she didn't mean it. "Just don't lock me out again. You said you were okay. It makes me feel like you don't want me around." The sadness in her daughter's eyes brought tears to her own.

"I never want you to feel like that, Miki, I'm sorry. I won't do it again."

Mikela nodded, smiled shyly. "Smells good in here."

"Been cleaning house."

"About time!"

"I know you said to wait a while, but I was dropping Miki off at school and it was early enough to stop by and Miki wanted to see you, and . . ." Giving her a cautious glance, Mike stopped, waiting for an answer.

"I'm glad you came."

"So you're still doing okay?" He didn't mention Asa, but the question was in his eyes.

"Like I said on the phone, things have changed." He gave a brief, knowing nod and she wondered how much he had guessed. Mikela was texting, but from past experience Jocelyn knew she had heard and noted every word.

"No more silver car? Guess we can hang out again." She glanced at Jocelyn over her phone, daring her to lie, and it took Jocelyn by surprise, how much her daughter had figured out. She glanced at Mike, who gave a slight shake of his head that said, we'll talk later—the way they always had.

"So where do you want to hang out?"

"Anywhere but here."

"Let's take this a step at a time, Miki, okay?" Although nobody had said it, Mike had become the custodial parent. Jocelyn realized then that she'd surrendered her parental rights; it would be a long time before she regained her daughter's trust. Would she *really* forgive her? Could she forgive herself?

"I feel like I've gotten over some kind of sickness," she muttered to Mike.

"You're still grieving for the loss of Miss Constance. Grief takes all kinds of shapes you didn't plan on. It did for me, too, when I lost my mom."

She shook her head with a slight, bitter smile. "This was more than grief, Mike."

"But it's over now."

"Yeah, it is."

"Why don't you get Luna to come by and burn some sage," he said, trying to lighten things up; he was good at that. Burning sage was one of Luna's trademarks that neither of them took seriously, but it felt good to chuckle about it together, to feel their connection once again.

"I'll ask her when she comes. She's supposed to drop off some papers that belonged to my great-grandmother."

"Caprice?" Mikela asked.

"You remember?"

"How could I forget?"

How could she? Jocelyn realized. Everything that had happened between them had begun on that October Sunday.

"I found some stuff that belonged to her in an old suitcase in the attic. Want to go through it with me?"

"The attic? You're serious about this cleaning thing aren't you, Mom?"

"Yeah, I am. And you know what else? You were right. Grandma was the one who copied all those old papers."

"All that beautiful cursive."

"All that beautiful cursive," she repeated thoughtfully, deciding in that moment that most of Caprice's pages should not be shared—even with her daughter. They were meant for Nana France's eyes alone, and she had decided not to read them; her mother's thoughts should stay buried with her.

May she live in peace away from the turmoil that I have brought on myself and take what is strong from me and destroy what remains.

Mikela threw her a warning look. "Mom, your mind is going somewhere else. Don't start acting weird again, okay?"

"Okay," she said, stronger, sure of herself.

Mike had a show later on that night and asked if he could drop Mikela off after school and pick her up around ten, and Jocelyn agreed that was fine. She wasn't ready for Mikela to move back home yet, and she sensed Mikela wasn't ready to come, but this was a good beginning.

And the thought of seeing her daughter again stayed with her and made her smile as she vacuumed the worn rug on the living room floor, and opened the door to the attic, finally ready to discover the gifts—or whatever they were—that remained.

ॐ

At five in the morning, the day after Jocelyn read Caprice's last pages, something shoved Luna out of bed straight down to the floor.

"What the hell was that?" she said, picking herself up.

There were no images in gray this time. No colors, smells, or sounds. Just a powerful push. And humming that wouldn't let her be, a buzzing noise that made her recall a charming, cunning voice she wanted to forget.

There is nothing you can do. You are helpless and she will hate you if you try to interfere. That's how much power I have.

Jocelyn had told her he was gone from her life, that it was over between them. (As if *he* were a normal man!) And she did sound stronger, more like herself. He'd left the country, Jocelyn said.

Luna knew better.

You don't have power when it comes to beings like me.

What was that Geneva had said about fire cleaning all? That Jocelyn should burn what once belonged to the lady. There were her papers, the ones she'd promised to return, but they were only copies. No power in burning them.

There must be something else.

Asa/Ezra/Demon/Incubus, he wasn't through with Jocelyn yet. Luna knew that with the clear certainty of the boon.

Pinto nuzzled her hand, and she got up to fill his bowl

251

with food and put water in the kettle for tea. There was no going back to sleep.

He had said those words after Jocelyn left him . . . before she *thought* she had left him.

Luna would wait until a decent hour before she paid her friend a visit. Come to drop off Caprice's papers, she would say, like Jocelyn's text had asked. That was as good an excuse as any.

And if she was lucky, the boon would tell her what needed to be done from there.

19

and sank her in the sea

The dust on the attic windows shut out the sun, leaving the room dim and uninviting, and Jocelyn shuddered when she entered. She picked up Caprice's carpetbag and tried again to take it downstairs, then changed her mind. It was heavy and too much for her to carry on her own. Constance had replaced a leaky section of the roof several months ago but not in time to rescue the satchel. The bag was dry, but mold had destroyed what time could not.

Still, Jocelyn was curious. She brought a hammer, screwdriver, and chisel up from the basement, and recalling Mikela's concerns about the locked screen door, checked again to make sure it was open. The memory of the light in Mikela's eyes when they hugged still made her smile. If there was anything worth sharing that belonged to Caprice, it would be fun to share it with Miki when she came by later, a bonding experience to begin repairing what had been lost. It would be a fitting tribute to Constance as well, sharing with her own daughter what they hadn't had the time to share with each other.

Rust had destroyed the lock, so prying it open was impossible. The upholstery around the leather straps was ripped, giving Jocelyn just enough space to peek inside the bag, but nothing could be seen. Eager to discover what was there, she tore away enough of the rotting fabric to allow her to shake some of the contents onto the floor.

A dozen soiled, mildewed handkerchiefs fluttered out. Were they the ones Caprice had mentioned in her pages? They'd been beautiful once, expensive linen, and despite their current state, she could make out the delicate daises and buttercups carefully embroidered on each one—whimsical flowers, made to thrill a child; Nana France's initial were stitched in each corner.

My handkerchiefs, scented with perfume, were all I was able to hide, Caprice had written. They had outlasted her.

Eager to see what else was hiding, Jocelyn shook the bag again, harder this time. Two dresses—one navy, the others gray—were lodged at its bottom, and she pulled them from their hiding place. They were dowdy things, aprons pinned on each, the kind worn by domestics or cooks, certainly not what Caprice would have worn to visit her only daughter—that outfit would have been colorful and chic, paid for with money saved for months. These belonged to the woman who had spent her last years cleaning and cooking for the ladies of the Haven of Mercy. These must have been sent later with Caprice's papers after she'd died.

Sheets of paper filled with writing and drawings were tucked into the bag's recesses, each slim bundle tied with black ribbons. (The work of the compassionate Haven ladies?) Mildew and mold had destroyed what had been written and drawn, and most of the images were impossible to decipher. Were these the originals of the papers Constance had copied, finding and copying them before they had been ruined? Jocelyn held one sheet to the dim light, making out Caprice's beautiful writing, now impossible to read. Constance, astute lawyer that she was, must have realized how delicate they were and copied them immediately to preserve what she could.

Like something Grandma would do.

One packet was filled with drawings and sketches and apparently not deemed important enough by her prose-loving mother to copy. Most had faded into nothing, too far gone to bother with, but a few were identifiable. Caprice must have been an artist in addition to being a writer, and that was worth celebrating.

He snatched away all things that brought me joy: the small drawings I sketched of you from memory, my bits of verse, my books of prose, my journals.

There were several sketches of a child. Nana France, perhaps, but faded, and it was difficult for Jocelyn to imagine her grandmother as a young child with braids and bows. Another was of a biracial woman with a stout man standing steadfastly behind her. Regina Heinz, the landlady she'd mentioned in those first papers, and her German husband. Tucked underneath those were several of elderly women, probably the women of the Haven of Mercy. They looked the part, with their kind, serious faces, hair drawn tight in no-nonsense buns.

One sheet of paper, thin and ragged around the edges, was folded in quarters, and Jocelyn opened it carefully so as not to tear it. There was little left to see on this one, except the eyes, and Caprice had managed to capture their intensity. Further down on the sheet was what looked like the sketch of a scar, but this was no portrait; there were no outlines to this drawing—no chin, lips, or neck. There was only a slight resemblance, Jocelyn told herself, as she quickly folded it back and tossed it on the floor, but her fingers shook, and a chill went through her.

The sound of the back door banging closed made her grin. Could Mike be dropping off Mikela? It seemed too early, so it must have been a half day at school. They did that on Mondays sometimes, a gift to teachers as well as students. In his rush to get her to school on time, Mike must have forgotten. But this was good; she needed to see them both again. An unexpected, delightful surprise.

"I'm in the attic," she yelled. "Got some stuff from Caprice to show you. I'm coming down!" She tossed everything back into the carpetbag and rushed down the stairs through the living and dining room and into the kitchen. She stopped short there, unable to move.

Asa stood in the kitchen, blocking the back door, which he'd left ajar. There was no way around him. A cold fist squeezed her heart, and she caught her breath. She made herself look over his head toward the treetops, the clouds in the sky—anything to keep from looking into his eyes. I will not let him frighten me, she said to herself. I will not let him frighten me.

"How did you get in?" She made her voice strong and forceful.

"Have you forgotten? I have the keys." He gave them a

little shake and placed them on the kitchen table. "Can I have mine back, too?"

"Of course, sure." She grabbed the key ring out of the pocketbook she'd left on the kitchen table, snatched his key away from the others, and tossed it beside hers. "Sorry, I forgot I had it."

"Jocelyn, what's wrong?"

"Nothing," she said quickly, defensively.

"You're acting . . . you're acting like you're afraid of me."

"I'm not afraid of you." She stepped backward, away from him and toward the stairs, angry at herself for showing him that she was. She took a deep breath, remembering that this was a way to banish fear. *Breathe in, breathe out. Breathe in, breathe out.* And why, she reminded herself, should she be afraid of anyone in her own damn kitchen, her own damn house. "No"—she lifted her head braver now—"why would I be afraid of you?" She forced a laugh, made herself shrug. "I'm just surprised to see you. You startled me, that's all. I thought maybe you'd left the country."

"Without saying good-bye? Come on, I know things are different between us now, but we're still friends, right? Kind of friends? A little bit friends?"

She made herself nod: It seemed silly not to.

"Good!" He grinned, relief clearly on his face, and his familiar, mellow voice put her at ease, assuring her she had nothing to fear—but suddenly she noticed his teeth; they'd turned as long and jagged as they were in her dream. Then, in an instant, his old smile was back, as charming as it had always been. "We've been through . . . well, I'm just sorry things ended like . . . well the way they did. Can I come in?"

"You're already in."

"Right." He nonchalantly made his way to the center of the room, leaning casually against the kitchen counter, and she remembered for a moment how good he was in bed, the feel of his fingers on her body, inside of her. She shook her head, violently chasing away the thought. "No, what? Why are you shaking your head no?" His voice was charming, beckoning.

"No reason." She dropped her eyes, fearful that by simply looking in her eyes he could undermine her resistance. What is wrong with me? she said to herself. Why does he have this effect? She had asked herself that question from the very beginning.

"Well, like I said, I'm sorry things ended like they did."

"I am, too," she said after a minute. No harm in giving him that, she decided. But then she noticed something in his left eye beside the scar; it carried the spark of malice. Just as quickly it was gone, and he was himself again, Asa, whom she had loved too deeply for her own good.

He smiled slightly, sadly. "Well, I'm glad to hear you say that. You mean—meant—a lot to me, Jocelyn, more than I think you understood, and well . . . whatever it was that I said that morning, I . . ."

"You know goddamn well what you said," she shouted, suddenly angry. His denial made her brave; rage and disappointment came pouring out. How dare he deny those horrible words? "You know what you said!"

"Let's not make this worse than it is." That demanding, authoritative tone was in his voice, the one she'd once found so attractive and masterful. He stepped toward her, reaching out to touch her.

"Don't!" She held up her hand to stop him.

"Oh, Jocelyn, don't be like that." He stepped closer; she took a step back.

"Okay, now, leave. We've said good-bye, isn't that why you came over?"

He cocked his head to the side, like he used to when he wanted to convince her to do something she didn't want to do, when he wanted to charm her. "Don't be like that, okay?" He backed away, letting her have her space.

"Why did you come? Didn't I make it clear I didn't want to see you again?"

He shrugged. "You know me, Jocelyn, and you actually didn't make it that clear. Not crystal clear. You just fucking ran away. Disappeared. I can't take no without being hit in the face by it. Don't you know that about me by now?"

"I don't know a goddamn thing about you by now, except you're probably crazy as hell. Isn't that what you are?"

His smile was slow and strangely inviting. "I'm anything you want me to be. Remember that?"

"I remember a lot of crazy shit you told me that day."

"And all of it is true."

"None of it is true!"

"You're too much of a coward to face it, to give me what I need from you. Just like before."

"Before?" Fear crawled up her back. "Okay, go! Get the fuck out of here! I'm sick of you!"

"Are you really?"

"Isn't that what I fucking said!"

"One more thing."

"What?"

He reached into his pocket and pulled something out. "I found this underneath the couch. It must have been hiding from us all those times we looked for it. Remember?"

Nestled in his palm was her earring, the diamond stud she had worn the first night they met, the one she hadn't seen, missed, or thought about since the morning Mikela asked about it.

"Remember?"

She knew he was referring not to the loss of the earring but what had happened between them in the weeks that followed, the lovemaking that had torn her body and mind asunder, and it all came back in a rush so hard and deep it snatched away her breath. The diamond glistened in his palm, calling her to it. Nana France's diamond that had always brought her luck.

"Well, come and get it," he said offhandedly. "And then I'll go."

She glanced up at him, not sure what to do. His palm was open and his fingers enticing her, like a trainer tempting a scared pony with a cube of sugar.

"Leave it on the table," she said.

"On the table!" He reared back, shook his head, and glanced at her incredulously. "So now you're afraid to touch my hand? Like I'm the golden goose in that old Grimm's fairy tale? The one where everyone who touches its golden feathers sticks to it, turns into a motley line of unfortunate losers trailing behind it? So now I'm the golden goose?" He looked genuinely hurt, and Jocelyn smiled despite herself. "I haven't asked you to kiss me good-bye. Just take your earring and I'll be gone."

"If you think I'm being silly, I don't care. I don't give a damn if you do."

He shook his head, slowly, thoughtfully. "No, you just don't trust me anymore, and I guess I can't blame you at this point."

"Yeah, you're right about that."

"But you know how I feel about you?" He stepped closer.

"So you're not going to be traveling?" she asked, changing the subject, not moving back.

He glanced away, avoiding her eyes. "Not sure yet." He paused. "I just realized something, Jocelyn. Except when we met that first day, this is the only time I've been in your place, after all these months. Nice kitchen."

"It works for me."

"What's upstairs?" he asked, glancing above his head. Until that moment, Jocelyn had forgotten the look that had come into his eyes when he'd glanced toward the stairway that first day. She considered asking him about it, then changed her mind. Just let it go, she said to herself, let him be on his way. Get him the hell out of here.

"Not much."

"When I first came in, I heard you say something about being in the attic, something about Caprice, your great-grandmother, right?" He was taunting her; amusement danced in his eyes.

"Stop playing games. Just give me my damn earring!" She moved toward him and snatched it away, her hand grazing his, and as she felt the soft nakedness of his palm, a spark of energy came between them, the delightful tension that had drawn and always held her.

His fingers crept over her fingertips, caressing her palm, then grabbed her wrist and traveled up her inner arm, elbows, shoulder, briefly touching her breast, gently squeezing her nipple, and finally roaming to the tender spot on her throat as he pulled her to him, holding her firmly, grazing her chin with his lips, settling into her mouth with his soft, brutal tongue.

She pulled away, excited yet repulsed, stunned and unable to move. And in that moment, the dream came back vividly, as if she were living it. The savage cruelty of the glint in his eyes, the arrogant thrust of his chin, the violence in his hands. As he pulled her toward him, she knew if she didn't get away she would be his for as long as he wanted her, just as he'd promised she would be, and that no one could pry her from his grasp. She knew it as clearly as Caprice must have known it.

Nothing was imagined; everything was true.

> He struck the top-mast with his hand,
>   The fore-mast with his knee;
> And he broke that gallant ship in twain,
>   And sank her in the sea.

"You really are that man, the one she loved, aren't you? You've come for me because you couldn't have her," she said, amazed by the incredulity of her own words.

He smiled slightly, not unkindly. "I told you that from the beginning, who I was. You just didn't listen to me."

She tried to pull away; he held her tight.

"And you are she," he whispered, his breath burning like steam against her cheek.

20

destroy what remains

It was the power of the Markham women—Bombay gin, burned biscuits, Chanel No. 5—the very bones of the house itself that wouldn't let him take her. All those who gave her life and breath helped push him off, and he landed hard on his hands and knees on her freshly scrubbed kitchen floor.

Jocelyn ran into the dining room, bumped into the heavy mahogany table parked in the center of the room with its six sturdy chairs, skirted its matching china cabinet stocked with rarely used Lenox china. The overstuffed sofa in the living room blocked her path to the stairway, and on the way up she tripped on one of Herman's well-worn Bokhara rugs. She heard Asa curse as he got up, walking not running, cocky as always, sure that he would get what he came for.

There can be nothing left of you but me. That is my condition.

She sprinted to the second floor—two, three stairs at a time—not looking back, out of breath, tripping once and then again, down the hall, passing Mikela's room and the bathroom with the stained tub Mikela hated, turning a corner to her room, her mother's room that had once belonged to Nana France. Would she find protection there? Hoping that somehow she would, she headed to it. But hope was irrational, and this was not the time for that.

The door was closed. She didn't remember closing it; she must have done it on her way down this morning—or maybe wind blowing in from somewhere, or the simple willfulness of the house itself. It had always had a mind of its own; she had no choice now but to follow its lead, go where it led her. She paused to listen but couldn't hear him. Had he stopped? Was he giving up, going back to wherever he had come from?

To take what was most precious to me and give it to him for our love. To cut my ties with everything mortal.

Like Marimba had done with her children.

A beautiful woman with frightened eyes that never seemed to smile.

What were their names, what had he told her?

Chance and Alma, named after the two things in life that decide your fate: luck and soul.

And what of the woman, Marimba? She had helped Caprice before, would she suddenly come to help her now? Or was she bound to him in stranger, stronger ways?

She heard him walk across the dining room, his shoes echoing on the hardwood floor. Biding his time, slowly and deliberately. He was in the living room now, beside the couch, footsteps muffled by Herman's thick rug, rounding the coffee table, heading to the stairs.

She backtracked down the hall toward the attic, so frightened her breath came in gasps, still feeling the mark of his fingers on her throat, the thickness of his tongue in her mouth. Why had she let him touch her? How had it happened? Had his mere presence made her vulnerable so quickly? She ran into the attic and tried to lock the door behind her, but the latch was broken, had been for years; there was never a need to fix it. Rushing up the steep, narrow stairs, she caught her foot on the edge of the ragged carpet; it held her until she shook herself free.

He was on the second floor. She stood and held her breath, pressing her body against the attic wall, afraid to go farther, afraid he would hear her. She heard him stop in front of her bedroom and try the door, but knocking first. "Are you in there?" he asked politely. "Are you in there, Jocelyn, hiding from me?" He opened it; she heard him step inside.

And what would she do when he caught her?

It would be quick, he told me, and I would be with him always. Like stepping through a door, into a place I would never leave.

If she went quietly into the depths of the attic, maybe she could hide from him. She took each stair slowly, holding her breath, afraid to let it go.

"Where are you now?" he asked, amused, as if they were playing some lethal game of hide-and-seek. It turned her stomach; she choked back vomit.

Something told her she would find safety in the attic—a place to hide, somewhere in the shadows. In the closet that held her father's clothing? In one of the steamer trunks? Stay there until he gave up and left.

You have given me the chance she took away and I can't let it happen again.

She ran into the dim space, her eyes adjusting slowly to the darkness. Caprice's bag was in the middle of the floor where she'd left it, and she tripped over it, scraping the palm of her hand on the rough-hewn floor. The cedar closet held her father's clothes, and she ducked into it, the dust making her sneeze as she moved deeper in. Old sleeves like fingers tickled the back of her neck; shoes piled high on the floor scratched her ankles.

One quick stroke, and it will be done, for all eternity. One stroke, or two, perhaps, to cut what holds you here.

They both knew what held her. It was as deep and enduring as the love Caprice held for Nana France, that Constance held for her. That tie would never be broken.

He was in the attic. She peeked out from between her father's jackets, the way Mikela used to do from Mike's when she was three—a scared kid hiding from the bogeyman. Except this one had a voice that could enchant and snatch a woman's soul.

He stood inside the doorway, his muscular body blocking it as he had the one downstairs, his face shadowed in the tiny slits of sunlight drifting in from the window above. Why had she never seen his evil before, the teeth pointed as his lips turned into an animal's snarl? She held her breath, sure he could hear her breathing. How many times had he told her he could hear her heart beat when he listened. He was listening now.

Jocelyn had always heard that hearts stopped when frightened, that one could feel a skipped beat—once, twice—until the rhythm returned. She knew that was true, because hers had stopped until her breath came back fighting its way out of her chest.

The trembling began in her shoulders, dropping into the small of her back, settling in a knot in her stomach. He could hear her heart, too, because he'd said he could hear such things. He would have heard it stop. He would know by the sound of her terror, and that would tell him where she was, and he would pull her from her hiding place. He could smell her fear like any stalking creature could. She took in a breath. One, two, three. Deep into her heart.

Please help me, now, she prayed. *Please help me!*

The trembling stopped.

Take what is strong and destroy what remains.

For so many years, Jocelyn had heard nothing about Caprice but tales of her weakness—her abandonment of Nana France, her cowardice, her running off with a crazy man who led her astray (and she knew now that man was not a man). And along with those came Nana France's accusations, constant as a chant: just like her, won't amount to pee.

And she believed them.

Caprice, the source of all sorrow in her family, the weak link in a chain of strong, able women. The foolish one who shamed them all. Yet Caprice had possessed courage and spirit, had fought for herself and her child in the only way she could. Without them knowing it, she had passed it down to Nana France and then to Constance and now it was hers.

Don't worry about the child, Connie, just a fever. It will break before evening and she'll be just fine.

They were here with her now, each in her own way; always had been.

Jocelyn knew what she must do. Caprice had run for her life, but she would not. She would find a way to defeat him, because she had two generations of Markham women behind her.

He stopped. She peeked from the closet and saw him tearing through Caprice's bag like a scavenger ripping the guts from a dead animal.

Jocelyn stepped from her hiding place. He glanced up at her, an odd, puzzled look on his face, then stood, moving toward her, Caprice's bag between them.

"I knew that you would not leave me again," he said.

A moment passed. Two. Three.

They heard it at the same time: a door slamming downstairs, someone running across the first floor, up the stairs to the second, toward the attic. Mikela? Home from school, coming upstairs to find her? With each footstep, Jocelyn's courage ebbed. It was no use. She knew in that instant that she would do anything he asked, go anywhere he took her, as long as he didn't kill her child.

"If I go with you, will you leave her alone?" she asked.

Asa's smile was as enchanting as it was deceitful, but there was evil in his eyes, a gravelly edge to his voice as hard as stone. "Come with me. Believe in me again, the way Caprice once did. Stay with me until my time with you is over. Do as she wouldn't." He came forward, reached toward her. Jocelyn stood still, unable to move as she listened for the voice of her child.

It wasn't Mikela but Luna who stepped into the room, dressed in white, filling the room with her blend of strong, powerful herbs.

"Don't let him touch you!" Luna's voice was calm, yet authoritative in a way that Jocelyn had never heard it. "That is how he controls you, with his touch." Stunned but obedient, Jocelyn stepped back, out of his reach.

Rage dissolved his face and he turned from Jocelyn to Luna, contorting his hands into brutal claws ready to tear her apart. Jocelyn, staring hard, could see nothing of the man she had known. Each part of Asa had become a distortion: the white polished teeth now sharply edged, the eyes filled with yellow fury, the beautiful skin mottled and gray as if he'd stepped from the grave.

"Burn anything that belongs to Caprice, burn it! Whatever it is, burn it now!" Luna screamed as he grabbed her, shaking her hard like a toy. Yet there was no fear in Luna's face, and her courage brought back Jocelyn's own.

Take what is strong from me and destroy what remains.

Nana France's lighter was still in her jeans and Jocelyn frantically dug for it, praying there was enough fluid left to do what she had to do. She clicked it, once, twice, and a tiny flame flickered. She grabbed the sketch Caprice had drawn of his eyes and held it against the tiny flame until it caught fire, then tossed it into the carpetbag. The other papers burned quickly, and as they did his eyes grew wide in disbelief. With a swift, violent motion, he tossed Luna behind him. Jocelyn heard her hit the floor.

But nothing happened, nothing had changed, and Jocelyn realized with a terrible anguish that Luna was wrong: the burning made no difference. She chanced a look at Luna, lying stunned and broken against the far wall, her breath coming in short, uneven bursts.

"Come now," Asa said, reaching for her. "You have no choice."

Then as swift and light as a breeze came the fragrance that had followed Jocelyn for months, but far stronger than she had ever known it. He smelled it, too, lifting his head, snorting it, gulping it like a dying beast gasping for air.

"Caprice?" His voice was a whining specter of itself.

The scent was everywhere—floating high near the window, around the wardrobe that held her father's clothes, past the crates of broken dolls and useless records; it hovered for a moment around her face, so strong, mingling with her breath as it finally settled around Caprice's still-smoking bag, cloaking the odor of burning fabric.

It was as if he could see it, the way his eyes followed the smell like it was a living thing. He stepped toward the place where it hovered. He put his hand out to touch it.

And that was when the house and all who dwelled within it took their final due.

Without warning or creak, the floor gave way beneath him. He sank straight down from the attic, through the ceiling of the second floor, to the first, and into the basement in a swirl of dust, dirt, and splinters. As he disappeared, he pointed at Luna, who lay wounded on the floor.

"You!" he screamed.

Neither woman spoke. It had happened in the blink of an eye—too quick to comprehend, to make sense of. Jocelyn was the first to move; finally able to catch her breath, she ran across the room to where Luna lay. Taking her friend in her arms, she held Luna tightly, comforted by her presence and the smell of sweet herbs she had worn to protect them.

"You okay, girl?"

"I'm fine," Luna said, painfully standing up. "He's gone?"

"Yeah, I think he is."

They went to the hole that had swallowed him and peered down, seeing nothing but dust, broken wood, and darkness.

"What should we do?" said Jocelyn.

"Besides pray? Nothing."

"Do you think he . . . his body fell into the basement? It looks like it goes that deep."

"No."

"Where do you think he went?"

"Wherever he came from."

"How do you know?"

"I just do," Luna said, with such certainty that Jocelyn didn't dispute her. "That hole will be the only trace of him left."

"Well then, I guess we'd better go downstairs and see how deep it goes," Jocelyn replied, and the two women, holding each other for strength, walked cautiously but fearlessly down the attic stairs.

The boon was right this time, not a trace of him remained. A carpenter, one of Luna's oldest, most loyal clients, made repairs the next morning. He shook his head in amazement, saying he'd never seen anything quite like it—a hole going straight to the basement destroying nothing in its wake. If he was looking for an explanation, he didn't get it.

"I guess these things just happen," Jocelyn said, smiling sweetly, paying in cash three times what he had asked.

Two weeks later, Mike brought Mikela home to stay, and stayed himself for chicken and dumplings. At Mike's request, Luna burned sage throughout the house—and when no one was looking, added a sprinkle of dried carnation petals for good measure.

While Mike helped Mikela unpack, Luna and Jocelyn shared a bottle of red wine, just as they had that October night so many months before.

"But how did you know what he was?" Jocelyn asked, broaching the subject that neither had mentioned since it happened. Luna shrugged and shook her head.

"Could have been all those damned vampire movies you claimed were warping my mind," she said, and they both laughed, recalling their afternoon lunch at Marley's Farm. "Best to try to forget the whole mess. There are just mysteries in life you simply can't explain."

"That sounds like such a cliché!"

"But it's true. Guess that's how it got to be one." Jocelyn nodded in agreement, and they sipped their wine in silence, then hugged like the good friends they were.

"At least it's over," said Jocelyn with a sigh of relief.

But Luna remembered Asa's voice when he screamed at her, the demon his face had become, the wrath of evil in his burning eyes—and the boon whispered it wasn't over yet.

"At least for now," she said.